YOU'RE SURE TO FALL IN LOVE

Again!

*for Mary
with thanks*

Brian C Beck

YOU'RE SURE TO FALL IN LOVE

a novel

by

BRUCE K BECK

AUDACITY BOOKS
WE DARE TO TELL THE TRUTH
New York

Also by Bruce K Beck:

Produce: A Fruit and Vegetable Lovers'
Guide (Friendly Press, 1984)

The Official Fulton Fish Market Cook-
book (E P Dutton, 1989)

This is a work of fiction. Names, characters, businesses, places, events, and
incidents are either the products of the
author's imagination or used in a ficti-
tious manner.

ISBN: 978-0-9991182-0-7

This is a first edition from Audacity Books.
Visit us on the web at www.audacitybooks.com
For information about rights or purchases,
please email us at info@audacitybooks.com.

For Walter Maas,
the best companion for all journeys

Old Cape Cod

If you're fond of sand dunes and salty air,
Quaint little villages here and there,
You're sure to fall in love with old Cape Cod....

Written by Claire Rothrock, Milton Yakus, and Irwin Pinkus,
introduced by Patti Page in 1957

How Little We Know

Maybe you're meant to be mine.
Maybe I'm only supposed to stay in your arms a while,
As others have done.
Is this what I've waited for, am I the one?
Oh I hope in my heart that it's so.
In spite of how little we know.

Written by Hoagy Carmichael and Johnny Mercer, introduced by Lauren Bacall in the film _To Have and Have Not_, 1944

As I look back, the freedom of that particular year, 1976, stands out in vivid relief, superimposed upon the horrors of the war in Vietnam, which had only just ended a few years before. Well, not ended, exactly, but at least there was a wonderful sense of release when the Paris Peace Accords were signed in January of 1973, even though the whole mess continued to simmer until the fall of Saigon in April of 1975. And never mind the suffering of the players—on both sides—in the aftermath. Those of us not directly involved were able to take a deep breath and start a new life. A new freedom. Hell,

Bruce K Beck

I even spoke to an Army recruiter one day and might have enlisted if they had promised me Special Services—The Entertainment Wing—which they could not. "This one's for the boys!" would have been easy for me. Combat training, not so much.

But don't let me get started on Nam or we'll never get to my story. Let me focus just on that one summer. That one delicious summer. I talked for years about constructing a history of it. Well, there isn't so much physical evidence—one small memento, a few photos in the public domain, a menu, a tiny piece of jewelry. No, this will not be a history. Instead it will be an honest story constructed from the building blocks of memory and perception.

Perhaps long-term memories are formed as the result of frequent rehearsal, repetition, or re-imagining of the event. And in this way tales can change, if nearly imperceptibly, in the retelling. Am I a reliable witness? Yes, I think so. Is this a documentary? No, far from it. It is my version of the stories, mine and those of a whole collection of people who lived and loved and sweated and strove and mostly survived that glorious summer of '76 in varying degrees of triumph or defeat. And then we were none of us ever quite the same.

New York City
2017

Chapter One

Easy Living

Living for you is easy living,
It's easy to live when you're in love,
And I'm so in love,
There's nothing in life but you.

Written by Ralph Ranger and Leo Robin for the film *Easy Living,* 1937,
popularized by Billie Holiday

At twenty-six, I was emotionally invested in maintenance. My
relationship, scarcely dry behind the ears, may have been only
a few months old, but it felt like a solid new core to be cherished, to be reinforced, to be protected at all cost. I found life
terrifying and thrilling in roughly equal measure, and in rough
proportion to the amount of gin or Scotch that I had downed.
I felt young, beautiful, talented, and special on one level. And
I also felt old, ugly, stupid, and worthless on another. So perhaps I was not unlike millions of other gay boys entering into
the remarkable year of 1976 CE. But I had found a man who
loved me, and who had an apartment in New York City, and
who had a real life with a career and friends and furniture. He

was also the most talented man I could ever meet. And so I was not prepared to do anything to put all of that at risk. Well, not prepared, true, but that doesn't mean that I was incapable of risk. In fact, I was just as good at stupid mistakes as the next child.

"What would you say to a summer on the Cape?" Bobby asked me that winter.

"Hmm. I don't really know much about it." Cape Cod, indeed. So what the hell did I know about Cape Cod, other than Patti Page and her tired lobster stew with an ocean view on the Ed Sullivan Show? Well, two tiny touches, actually. The first was an event from more than twenty years before, around the time I was born (even before Patti Page shilled for the Cape) that had nothing to do with me. That strip of sand had provided a haven for my favorite aunt and uncle. The ramp-up to the Korean War reactivated the draft and put their future in jeopardy because of my uncle's reserve status post-WWII. These two life-long Republicans fled their lives in New Jersey and hid out on the Cape. So they said. For six months? A year? Family stories like this are often vague. Not exactly Pilgrims, but?

I used to imagine my uncle receiving a phone call from his mother. "Charlie, it's your mother. You have a letter here. Do you want me to open it?" Did my favorite uncle get a draft notice, and if so, when his mother phoned, long distance, to read it to him, did he thank her politely (for he was always courtly with his mother in the years that I knew them) then hang up and say, "Fuck it! I won't go!" There is no one living to ask for these details, so I guess I have to let it go.

Recent events had made that story resonate with me because I had been busy with my own draft dodging, though of the less adventurous sort: college deferments and favorable lottery numbers. Nothing so glamorous as a disappearing act. But living with terror as an underlying emotion was a condition I understood. Perhaps I had always understood that kind of fear. To gay boys it is as natural as mother's milk.

And my other brush with Cape Cod, more concrete, is that without having actually visited it, I had seen it once. One morning a few years before, in my student days, flying home from London by way of New York, I looked out the window of the plane through an atmosphere of crystalline clarity down upon Cape Cod. Bam! There it was below us, a big sandy arm complete with flexed biceps, just as pretty as you please. No Google Map will ever be as handsome, nor as accurate. And never, in all my flights and all my destinations, have I felt a keener sense of place. So despite my ignorance, I had a positive reaction to the concept of spending time there.

"Jan Cooper called and asked me to write some special material for his summer season in Provincetown. He bought an old guest house with a nightclub downstairs. He does the evening show and has other performers in for a few weeks at a time to play the late show. And then he said, 'Why don't you come for the summer and conduct for me, and your sweetie can work as a waiter. I have a room for the two of you. You have to share the john, but it's right across the hall.' Well, the money's not great, but with both of us working it should be okay. And the Cape is so pretty. It might be fun. So what do you think, Sunshine?"

Jan Cooper! I had met him, once, backstage after a performance in New York. I had loved the show, had found him very funny and very skilled at his impressions. But it never occurred to me that I might spend a summer working for a famous drag queen, and in the foremost gay Mecca of the Twentieth Century. I'm not saying I was trepidatious, just that it seemed so unlikely.

"Sure. Let's do it!" I said.

That was the easy part. Committing to an adventure is easy for twenty-somethings. But Bobby was twenty years older, with an established career. Then came all the questions and arrangements and details, the transportation, all of it. I wondered, "Can you really get away from New York for three months without screwing up something important?"

"Well, the auditions for Ford's Theatre are coming up in early May, so the casting will be done, and the production meetings, too. I'd have to do some work in the afternoons while we're away, to make sure I'm ready. Rehearsals start September 12. We'll be home just after Labor Day, so it looks good."

"As long as it works for you, let's go for it."

This was just one more in a series of wonderful surprises that all started with my meeting Bobby James in Chicago the November before. The whirlwind courtship, my move to New York—it all happened so fast. And yet the routine of daily life in New York had settled in so easily, as if we had been doing it for years. The intimacy, the openness and honesty—it had all flowed simply, with no forced issues. Life was easy. Earning a living, as always, was not. Three months on Cape Cod followed by a month back home in New York, then three months in DC. At this rate I could defer grownup decisions for a very pleasant span. Yes, more honeymoon and less real life. Yes!

I probably shouldn't admit it—in the interest of sounding like a credible witness—but I also have this thing about water. A fortune teller had told me a few years before that I must always live near water, that I draw my strength from it. Like Scarlett O'Hara and the red earth of Tara, I guess. When the psychic told me this, I thought back to my favorite times from childhood, at Boy Scout camp on a huge lake, or at the coast on family vacations. The pronouncement came just as I was about to head off to study in Venice, which was of course a transformative experience. And then after college there was a tiny basement apartment in Chicago a few doors from Lake Michigan, followed by my new home in Manhattan a half-block from the East River. I was certainly all-in with water, and an entire summer on Cape Cod Bay sounded like a happy addition to my roster of favorite water memories.

Meeting Bobby James—a block from Lake Michigan—was the event that set my life on its present course. He was a handsome little man, perfectly proportioned, with a wicked smile, a cute butt, and a very nice package. His black hair was at least 50% white by the year we met, and he kept it short and boyish. Bobby smelled of lemon with a hint of musk, and it was a warm, inviting scent that made me eager to get close to him. He was very physical, and he loved touching my skin. I loved being touched, and so our mutual explorations were joyous.

In late 1975, Bobby had a gig in Chicago, for the month of November. We met the first Saturday night at an after-hours club. He came home with me and never returned to the apartment the owner of the club had given him, except to change clothes. Right away we both sensed that there was something important happening. And by the end of November, there was no question that I would finish up my life in Chicago and start a new one with Bobby in New York. And it seemed that we were working toward—dare I say it?—an unconditional love.

Chicago can be a great place to live. The arts are strong, and the food is exceptional and varied. I liked it very much, and one of my chief pleasures, other than the opera season at Lyric, one of the world's great opera companies, was WFMT radio. It brought me not only fine music (from Mozart to Judy Collins to Leadbelly) but Studs Terkel interviews and stories, and commentary from Claudia Cassidy, the legendary Chicago Tribune arts critic. And I miss all of that to this day. But my life was incomplete.

As an example of what I decided to give up when I met Bobby, let me tell you about one Saturday night earlier in the year. I met a guy in a dance bar, I guess, and went home with him. He was quiet, slim, sexy, and interested in me. His apartment was unusual in a '70s high-tech sort of way. It was outfitted with sensors that turned on lights when one walked into a room (and presumably turned them off again when one exited). And the ceiling over his bed was mirrored. Truly. It

6

has never occurred to me to mirror the ceiling over my bed, in any apartment, but this one time I found it charming and gave in to the impulse to enjoy it.

By late-night-drunken-sex standards, it was exceptionally good. I got so into it that I rimmed the guy. Which I do not ordinarily do. We finished, we slept. The next morning, we had a little Sunday morning coffee and a bite of toast and jam—hell, maybe he cooked an egg for me, but I'm not sure— and then we got into his car and he drove me to the garage where they were charging the battery on my old VW. We exchanged names and telephone numbers. I never phoned him. He never phoned me. I never saw him again. It was a wonderful encounter. It was, also, not enough.

Enter Bobby James with an offer of a permanent relationship. I jumped at it with both hands. Bobby and New York in one trim package. I never looked back. And then, there we were preparing to start a new summer adventure in Provincetown, Massachusetts. And I was enchanted.

Chapter Two

A Room with a View

. . . A room with a view,
And you,
And no one to worry us,
No one to hurry us through
This dream we've found. . .

Written by Noël Coward for the Broadway review *This Year of Grace*,
1928

It took me decades to learn to pack. I've gotten pretty good
at it in recent years, but in the summer of 1976 I was still
schlepping around far too much stuff, and without the benefit
of a wheelie, at that. Bobby also packed a lot for our Provincetown summer, but he needed it more than I: He needed
tuxedos for "work clothes," and note pads and music manu-
script, pencils and a sharpener, portable tape recorder, all that.
Foolscap pads and Black Wing pencils—hmm, hadn't thought
about them in years, and yet they were standard equipment in
those days.

I was still using my brown American Tourister hard-shell

bags from college. Bobby had a large folding bag, what you might call a valpack I suppose, though really huge. He called it "the mobile home." And there was also a soft-sided leather bag made of elephant hide that Bobby always felt a bit guilty about. Quick to declare that he never bought it, that a friend had gone out to Bloomingdale's to find him a new bag while he was packing for an important business trip, he nevertheless cherished "the elephant" for its elegance and toughness, capacity, and practical value. Except for the practical part, not so different from Bobby himself, I thought, as I was writing this.

We traveled on the Monday before Memorial Day, and it also happened to be Bobby's birthday, so we were in a holiday humor. We took advice from friends and booked the train to Boston. I happen to love trains—or used to, anyway—so four hours with Amtrak was easy enough. And then we took a cab to the ferry dock. It was a beautiful day, so the boats were running on schedule. Luggage in, ninety minutes on the open water, docking, luggage out and into a waiting taxi, all without a hitch.

Arriving at the Pilgrim House, I was charmed by its weathered clapboard exterior and slightly ramshackle mien. Bobby seemed a bit less cheerful about the whole thing. But together, we jumped headlong into our little pilgrimage, pulling our too-many bags from the taxi and carrying them up the steps to the front door. Richie met us at the door, Richie Sullivan, Jan Cooper's old friend, dresser, and fixer. He was in his thirties then, I think, and had worked for Jan for at least ten years. Richie was chunky and not a bit pretty, but he had a pleasant smile and a friendly way about him. "What a nice man!" I thought. Richie was always so calm and solid, so effortlessly efficient. Just the ground-wire that Jan needed in his flighty show-biz existence. Richie grabbed two bags and led us to our room at the far end of the ground floor hallway.

And so we entered for the first time our summer home, our little room with a view—of the parking lot, as it turned out. But it was a nice, quaint parking lot. And our proximity to the back door of the Pilgrim House meant that we could scoot out without encountering the entire household, which would prove to be a blessing as the summer progressed. It afforded us a semblance of privacy where little existed.

The room was sparsely furnished with old furniture, basic white sheets, a chenille bedspread, and flowered sheers at the windows. It was truly drab, and small, but we dragged all our bags in and set about industriously to get our new home set up for a summer of living and working.

When we had put away as much of our stuff as would fit into the closet and dresser, and under the bed, we repacked the balance, the things we might not need so soon, in our suitcases and headed up the hall to the kitchen. It was an ample country kitchen, roomy, welcoming, a real family kitchen for the resident family, not for transients. Complete with cat. A very large cat named Daphne. She was so large that Bobby declared her the Kate Smith of cats. And so he began to plan a nightclub act for her—*When the Cat Comes over the Mountain, Cat Bless America*, that sort of thing.

Jan walked into the kitchen just after we did. He greeted us warmly and welcomed us to Pilgrim House. There were hugs and kisses all around, and the usual banter: "How was your trip? You're on time, so I guess you weren't blown off course. Maybe next time. You two are the first to arrive. The others get in mostly tomorrow morning." Having only met Jan just once before, backstage in New York, I had no idea what to expect from him in "real life." Jan was fiftyish then, but he seemed older somehow—short and thick in the middle. He was largely devoid of theatricality offstage, but even in civvies he could not hide the twinkle in the eye and the quicksilver face that made him so devilishly funny onstage. I liked him immediately, but I could not help but wonder if some of his Red Skelton-like sweetness was not as suspect as Red Skelton's. Perhaps the summer would tell.

Looking back, I am shocked to realize that we survived the entire summer with little or no television. That would seem impossible now. Neighboring businesses had TV, but we got our news mostly from word-of-mouth and the Sunday New York Times. And this was before Ted Turner launched his first movie channel, so late-night entertainment on TV would have been mostly reruns of Perry Mason. The activities we chose instead were much more entertaining. There was a radio in the kitchen, but I don't remember its ever being switched on except for monitoring the weather. Certainly not for entertainment.

Richie showed us where to stow our suitcases. Luckily, there was a storage room under the stairs with enough space for all the extra stuff, and access whenever we needed something that did not fit into the room. When we returned to the kitchen, Jan was making coffee, and the four of us sat at the big round table to enjoy it. Jan also produced a coffeecake, which was actually pretty good. I've always loved pecans, so it was an easy sell. "Hot Buns Bakery," Jan said. "They're just down Commercial Street. Those dykes can really bake!" Now that the source of Jan and Ritchie's thick tummies was apparent, I made a mental note about being sure that the same thing didn't happen to me.

"Whenever you're ready, I'll show you the Madeira Room," Jan said. "Bobby, I hope you won't judge us too harshly when you see the piano. It won't hold its tune too well in this climate, but there is a good tuner in town, and we can have him in whenever you think."

"As long as it has eighty-eight keys," Bobby answered politely. He had played so many instruments over the years that one more bad one was not going to throw him.

"If eighty-eight is your wish, then eighty-eight it shall be," Jan assured him. Well, not Jan exactly, but someone more like Bette Davis. I found the imitation process fascinating to watch. Which was good, because I was to see a *lot* of it that summer.

We followed Jan and Ritchie down the creaky old back stairs. Jan switched on the work lights when he got to the bottom of the stairs, and then we caught our first glimpse of our new work home. The Madeira Room was a basement with seating for about sixty people, maybe eighty on a Saturday night. The neat little stage, framed by heavy dark-red velvet curtains, was flanked by a small space stage left for the "band"—a trio usually—and on the other side by a door leading backstage: two small dressing rooms, and a space for Jan's

13

costume storage and quick changes. The bar and the cashier's station were in the back of the house, near the main entrance from the street. And that was it.

I loved seeing the Madeira Room for the first time on a quiet afternoon when it was still boarded up. It had the faint odor of ancient lumber, creosote, and beach houses that have been shuttered for the winter. Once it came alive, filled with boys and booze, it might have been a cabaret anywhere. But when it was dark and quiet before opening, especially that first week, it seemed an organic part of the Cape that could never be duplicated in any other locale, so site-specific that it might crumble to dust if it were moved elsewhere.

I didn't ask anyone at the time, why Madeira? I didn't know yet that many of Provincetown's Portuguese families were originally from the Madeira Islands. I didn't know that the traditions of fishing and seafaring that seemed so much a part of P'town had their roots across the Atlantic. I didn't know a lot of shit. But then, as now, I was at least making an effort to correct that. Fitting, somehow, to slap the name Madeira onto the old hotel basement. I would have done the same.

With our introductions to the hotel and the Madeira Room out of the way, we returned to our room, settled in, made love, took a nap, and then headed out for an early supper. There was a small restaurant right in front of the hotel, Plain & Fancy. It was strictly plain, actually, but homey and welcoming, and the bar had cocktail onions for Bobby's vodka Gibson martini. So things boded well for our summer, considering that food and drink were waiting for us right in the front yard.

But it was not so easy, actually. Later that night we both began to feel a bit queasy. No awful retching, mind you, just that heavy feeling when the digestion is off. We chalked it up to travel nerves. The two older women who owned the Plain & Fancy were so nice that I hate to say this, but they are probably dead by now (and the restaurant is definitely gone), so I hope no one will mind if I tell you that the queasiness followed subsequent visits as well. So, we began to limit our Plain & Fancy trips to the bar, only. And after all, Provincetown had many adventures in store, culinary and otherwise.

Chapter Three

Let's Do It

. . . Cold Cape Cod clams, 'gainst their wish, do it,
Even lazy jellyfish do it
Let's do it, let's fall in love. . . .

Written by Cole Porter, introduced by Irène Bordon in the musical Paris, 1928

Bobby was used to forming new families for new shows. It was second nature to him to fall in love with a whole new group of people, only to leave them at the end of the production. Some he might never see again. And with the ones that did pass through his life again, he could pick right up where the old friendship had ended, without missing a beat. I was just beginning to learn about all of this, and I never did get the hang of it. Never have.

The morning of our second day in P'town, we were having coffee with Jan and Ritchie in the kitchen when the first addition to our new family arrived, one of Jan's dancers. He would also prove to be my favorite. Rand Geoffrey Ball III was a lively fellow-Southerner, slightly my junior. Lucy, many people called him, inevitably. I couldn't bear to call a cute guy Lucy, and he will always be Randy to me. When I think back on him, I always remember that much later when Bobby and I happened to be discussing him, Bobby observed, "You know, Randy has a lot of energy and a great ass. And that's really all it takes to succeed." I couldn't argue the point.

Randy's boyfriend had driven him up from New York, in a Buick Skylark the same year and color as my mother's! The boyfriend—whose name I can't seem to remember—was young and slim, nice looking, and had a winning smile. He stayed for a few days before heading home, and then would drive up for occasional weekends and holidays, so we got to see him a fair bit that summer. His easy charm was always a fun addition to the mix.

"Well cock-a-doodle-do! I can't believe we have another Southern belle here," Randy said to me. "I can tell already you don't smile enough, though. Smile, Magnolia!" Randy went into his best Cap'n Andy from *Showboat*. Of course he coaxed a broad grin from me instantly. A broad grin for me, that is. For some others it might be more a bemused smile. But the feeling of abandon was genuine. "I guess I'll have to call you Nolie," Randy declared. And so he did.

The next family member we met was Heath Woodford, the handyman (read building engineer), who stopped by with an update for Jan about the condition of the building and what it would need before opening. Heath was just over six feet tall, and looked strong and capable. And his T-shirt fell softly over a tightly-muscled torso that seemed to say, "This body does not go to the gym. This body is work-made." Heath smiled shyly and shook our hands. His grip was powerful but gentle. *Beauty and modesty in one package,* I thought. *Nice!* Later, Bobby said, "If I ever have any problems with my plumbing, I will certainly know who to call."

When Heath had left the kitchen, to get on with his work day, we all sighed a bit. Jan said, "Isn't he something? And such a sweetheart, too. I don't know what I'd do without him!" Jan batted his eyes and fanned himself for effect.

Randy said, "Careful, Jan. You don't want Heath's husband to find out about your affair."

"It's my affair, thank you very much," Jan replied.

As the day progressed, others arrived. One was Len Bloomer, Jan's other dancer (and one of only a handful of straight people we spent the whole summer with). Another was a very cute little blond boy who would be running a tiny lunch stand that opened onto the veranda of the hotel. His hair was so soft he looked like a chick newly hatched. And I found out later that he made great tuna sandwiches. Later that afternoon Jan's director/choreographer and his boyfriend arrived. They were both really nice guys, but I'm not going to tell you anything about them, because our interactions with them after the first week were slight, and I've forgotten both of their names, anyway.

In fact, there were all sorts of people that summer we had brushes with, including lots of showbiz people, some fairly fancy celebrities among them. One became known as The Queen of (Manhattan) Cabaret; one starred on Broadway two years later, when her husband and musical partner died the day before opening night; one had a long and successful television career; and there was a trio of musical comedy boys who entertained regularly in New York clubs for the next decade. But there is no point in my throwing a whole bunch of characters at you, when what I really want to do is tell a particular story. So I will try to give you just the information you need.

Jan arranged a get-together for Wednesday evening so that everyone could meet, have a drink, check out their equipment, and kick off the new season with everyone on board. Randy and Boyfriend came, the director and *his* boyfriend, of course, Ritchie, Len, and Heath.

Bobby greeted Don Walker, his new bass player, who seemed nice enough, and Liz Frankle, the drummer. Liz was a real live wire—a party animal, I suspected—and she seemed a perfect complement to her lover Heidi Gibson, who was very quiet. It turned out that Heidi was Heath's best friend, from their Halifax childhoods. When they talked together, I was shocked to see how much they looked alike. Heidi could easily have been Heath's little brother, so strong was the resemblance. And they shared a shy reserve that seemed to reinforce the appearance of siblinghood.

The wait staff all arrived during the first hour. "We're the Four Js," the first one told me. He was Jim, the bartender. Jim Beere was his name. And it was, of course, always good for a chuckle. Then the other three Js arrived almost simultaneously. They were just the sort of nice-looking young gay boys you would expect if you went to Central Casting and ordered up some waiters for the summer season in Province-town.

Jeff, Jerry, and Josh, were their names. One was prettier, one was hotter, one was smarter. Otherwise they seemed pretty much interchangeable to me. They were all on their third or even fourth season at the Madeira Room. The Js were quick to explain that they had previously been *Five* Js. The fifth had been bumped this summer to make room for me. So I was already feeling a little off balance when who should arrive but the fifth J himself.

Jake was his name, and the others seemed pleased that they had invited him to the party. I was not so sure. Jake Holman had found a job as a houseboy in a guest house to replace the job that Jan gave to me. So he would be around for the whole summer. Jake was a very cute guy, quick, energized. He was a little shorter than I, maybe a touch taller than Bobby, with dark hair and dark blue eyes. There appeared to be an exceptionally beautiful little body not well hidden by his shirt, as far as I could tell. Now, I don't read auras, but in Jake's case I sensed a Technicolor disaster the moment I clapped eyes on him. And I hated him immediately. Mostly I hated that he obviously resented me, as did the four other Js, or so it seemed. So this was to be the structure of the whole summer season? Ouch!

Introductions went all around, and then Jake said to Bobby, "Bobby James, no shit! I know you! I mean, I did some shows with Dennis Campbell in Boston, and I know he worked for you a few seasons in Chatham. I always suspected that every arrangement he gave me to play was actually yours!"

"That sounds like Dennis," Bobby answered.

So Hot Stuff is a musician, maybe even a talented one, and he knows all of Bobby's work and feels that they are like old friends. Should I slit my wrists now or later? I wondered.

Jake said, "I'd love you to hear me play some of your material, and maybe you could show me what you are working on now."

"Great," Bobby said. "There's a lot going on now before opening, but next week we could meet here some afternoon. There won't be anyone around to bother, so you can play whatever you like.

"Oh, thanks, Bobby. Next week, then. Looking forward!"

Then, to my surprise, Jake had a word for me. "You were a fat child, weren't you?"

"Yes, but how did you know?" I asked.

"So was I. There's something in the way we carry ourselves. I can always spot it." Now, the only quality in Jake's carriage that I could identify was sex, and I doubted that I presented the same way. But I had to give him credit for his insight.

In a very welcome change of pace, Jan took us to the bar and introduced us to the house cashier, Anita Lopes. Anita was about fifty, getting a bit broad in the beam, with a really kind, pretty face. Her light blue eyes sparkled as Jan carried on about how he couldn't run the club without her. "Save that performance for the stage," she told Jan.

"Now you behave yourself, Sunshine, and don't give Anita any trouble this summer," Bobby advised me.

"That's so cute!" Anita said. "But Sunshine is Bobby's

special name for you. I think I'll call you Sunny, if that's okay."

"Sure," I replied. And so she did.

A late arriver was an ample and highly singular creature called Bunny Babbit. "Drag Queen" is not the right term for what Bunny had created. He was more a force of nature than that, a grand pan-sexual Black presence. There was glamor galore, mind you. Gown, wig, makeup, jewelry. Once later on, when we had built a friendship, I told him his persona was Mae West meets Moms Mabley. Bunny was not amused by my observation, perhaps not so much because he found it in-apt as because he preferred originality to comparisons. And that, of course, is what he was: authentic and entirely original.

"Where are you from, little White boy?" the stately Black queen demanded.

"North Carolina," I replied.

"Well, I must say you look like a tasty little cracker. If a bit dry. We can fix that. You may assume the position." Bunny extended his right hand in a grand gesture, palm down. His theatricality scared me a bit, but there was no mistaking that this was not an offer of a handshake. Somehow I realized that I was meant to "kiss the ring." There were at least five large rings on his plump hand to choose from, but I went for the huge moonstone attached to his ring finger. I bowed from the waist crisply, and offered obeisance in a quick gesture of labial respect. Apparently, I got it right.

"Yes, you will do. Now, go away, Miss Saltine, and bring me a large Southern Comfort on-the-rocks." That was our first meeting, and that is how I always remember Bunny. Always will.

The last of our little family to arrive was Anita's husband, Moises Lopes. Indeed, he arrived at the Madeira Room every night to walk Anita home, so I was to see him often that summer. Moises was a burly man with strong Portuguese features, his wavy hair more salt than pepper those days. At first, I found him a bit gruff, even slightly menacing. But by our second or third meeting I realized that he was really a nice guy, and much friendlier than I had supposed on our first meeting. Moises was one of those men who smile rarely, but when they do, the smile adds a sudden radiance that is as dazzling as it is unexpected. Watching Anita and Moises heading home at night, I admired their bond, the affection forged through years of shared history. Perhaps I envied the comfort of it. I wondered, *Will Bobby and I earn that kind of love?*

After lots of laughter and too many drinks, the party broke up, and Bobby and I headed back to our room. He felt that things were going well. His rehearsal with his musicians had made him feel optimistic, and I tried to share his optimism, for his sake. But I was not so sure. Jake was galloping through my brain, as if on horseback, with the other Four Js riding in his wake. *I'll bet he looks good on horseback. I'll bet he looks even better bareback.* I needed sleep, and it didn't seem likely. I discovered that I had something else in common with Scarlett O'Hara: *No, I can't think about that now. I'll think about that tomorrow*, I decided. And eventually, it worked

Chapter Four

Perfect Stranger

. . . Perfect Stranger, my prince of romance,
Should I take a chance, or run away?

. . . Once you're no longer a stranger to me
Will you half so perfect be?
Is the perfect stranger smiling, or is he laughing at me?

Written by Bart Howard for the Julius Monk review *Take Five*, 1956

"I never met a dick I didn't like. Truly." Bunny's cocktail show was off and running. Bunny Babbit giving a nod to Will Rogers seemed so incongruous, I let loose a belly laugh that mixed with all the others in the room. People seemed to enjoy having a drink and a laugh at 5:00. It sure beat the news. I learned as the season went along that attendance was generally good, even on weekdays, and fans came back for more. It was a tribute to Bunny's showmanship and his humanity that people who were staying in P'town for a week might come to see Bunny two or even three times. He had lots of material, but even the same old routines were a treat to hear over and over.

25

That was fortunate for me, because I worked Bunny's cocktail show about half the time. Jan's big show at 7:00 I worked six nights a week, and then about half the time I worked the 9:00 show as well. That way, we waiters all had a chance to enjoy an early supper now and then, or a night out on the town. And roughly equal tips.

Bobby played only Jan's 7:00 show, so we managed to share an early dinner three or four nights a week, and a late supper most others. And then the rest of the time we had to ourselves. In those first weeks we went out occasionally, but often we stayed in, in our little room with a view. Neither Bobby nor I was a Biblical scholar, but we certainly knew our Hebrews 13:2: "Be not forgetful to entertain strangers: for thereby some have entertained angels unawares." While not exactly our motto, it was certainly a theme of the summer of '76. There were angels who passed through our little room, I have no doubt of it. And devils. And mere mortals as well.

Pilgrim House had an Open Door Policy. If the door was open, that meant the tenant was receiving—or giving, or some combination of the above. Or, to put it another way, open doors meant open arms.

"So what's it like to live in a candy store?" you ask me.

"Sweet!" I reply.

"Does it cloy?" you wonder.

"Yes, somewhere into the second month," I answer. But before that saturation point, before it starts to feel a bit repetitious, the availability of ready, random, randy sex is delicious indeed. Everyone deserves to experience at least a brief period of such abandon and fun. I suspect we were the last generation to have that kind of freedom. Pity. Humanity is resilient, though. People always invent another way. I am just glad that I lived my salad days in the all-the-dick-you-can-eat era. It was splendid.

After work on Memorial Day, Bobby and I came upstairs from the club, went to our room, took off our clothes, and settled in. "The hotel is at full capacity this weekend," Bobby reminded me. "There are some really hot guys staying here."

"Hmm. . . I wonder what they're doing tonight," I answered.

"Should we find out?" he asked.

"That would be the neighborly thing to do," I said, and made my way to our door. I opened it just a bit, at first, and peeked into the hall. No one about. But then, armed with a double Scotch, I opened the door wide and looked back to the bed, where Bobby gave a shrug and settled in for whatever might follow. I joined him. We had decided that it was permissible to add a third musketeer from time to time, as long as everything stayed one-for-all-and-all-for-one.

Within five minutes we had our first nibble. A really hot tall blond guy looked in, hesitated for a moment, and then gave a little wave and a nod as he disappeared. "At least he's polite," Bobby said. We had no illusions about being to everyone's taste, so a certain level of rejection was expected. The next stranger liked what he saw, walked in, and closed the door behind him.

Now, it was only in the first few weeks, before things began to feel a bit complicated, that Bobby and I were able to relax into some very nice late-night hedonism. I am going to pluck a few of those encounters out of the time-line, and out of context. Because they were so delicious, mostly, and because I hope you will enjoy hearing about the uncomplicated times that dotted our landscape. So the rest of this chapter is just for those who like to read graphic sex talk. You know who you are.

One of our most memorable visitors had a god-like form. He was what I now call "one of those tall thin Black guys who are all shoulders and tits." This one, like many others in the category, also had a truly glorious penis. I did my best to worship it in an appropriate manner, focusing my total attention upon the pleasure of this divinity, who seemed, at once, the perfection of flesh and not quite entirely of this earth. It was all I could do to share the duties with Bobby, for I felt competent to perform the service alone. The worship was completed well and truly. We exchanged the sacramental fluids. Our ebony idol disappeared into the night, leaving Bobby and me flushed and giddy in our bed. We never saw him again.

One night a rather nondescript little guy with a nice smile walked into our room, so we welcomed him. As I removed his shorts I realized that he had not only a perfectly nice dick, but a pair of beautiful balls. Everyone who knows me knows that I have an especial fondness for balls. Now, here is the existential dilemma about balls (even more so than about penises): they are poised there, like ripe, delicious fruits begging to be plucked, and yet we must be content to mouth them only. To consume them fully as we would wish would be an act of craven destruction. We must leave them intact so that the seed survives and flourishes, so that we may return to them again, or so that others might enjoy the blessings of their sweetness. If you have ever been served *animelle* (bull balls), you know there is a finality, a sadness about that rich meal. It's delicious, but not quite right, somehow. If I ran an abattoir I would bury those balls with full honors. It seems only fitting. But I digress.

That night I went pearl diving while Bobby focused more on the top half of our guest. In time, my focus broadened beyond my ball obsession, and before I knew it I had gone well beyond those slippery orbs to the crevice below. I don't do that very often, as you know, but it felt right. It seemed to feel right to our guest, too. As he eased his legs onto my shoulders in a gesture of confidence and surrender, I rose to the occasion. I set the pace, as the coxswain, as we fell into a natural rhythm and our little crew rowed on. Bobby at the bow amply filled the fore while I, at the stern, filled the aft and called the stroke. We rowed with precision for what seemed like a very long time, until I began to feel an orgasm on the way. And so did Bobby. And so did our guest. And so the three of us crossed the finish line together in a remarkable feat of victorious brotherhood. Our guest seemed just a tiny bit awed by the experience, as did we. He stayed for a drink and a kiss. Then, he dressed (put his shorts back on) and went away. We never saw him again.

Some of the sex was, well, potentially a little creepy. It was easy to avoid overweight guys in stained jockey shorts when they were sprawled out on their own beds just beyond their open doors. But when they found their way to *our* open door, it was sometimes easier to follow the laws of hospitality and invite them in, rather than risk bad manners. One night after work hours—visiting hours never ended—we were a bit unnerved to see at our door a huge reddish-colored guy with a large dark birthmark on the left side of his face. *At least his shorts look clean*, I thought. We invited him in, weakly, and poured him a drink while I kept hoping he would survey us at closer range and change his mind. He did not. The encounter that ensued was much more fun than either Bobby or I could have imagined at the start. Our out-sized Cro-Magnon turned out to be rather sweet and funny, and affectionate in a temporary sort of way. I always remember that he smelled of oranges. He also topped me with his great hulk and filled me deeply and well. So, it turned out to be a successful encounter despite the doubtful beginnings. We never saw him again.

There was really only one of our shared sexual encounters in our little room that summer that went really badly. I guess I must have thought about this one a lot, because I even remember the guy's name. Doug was a tall and skinny red-head with a long and skinny dick to match. I should mention that I have a soft spot in my heart for red-heads because I got my first case of crab lice from a red-head. Some things you just never forget. But on this occasion, as the sex got underway, Doug began to develop a strong crush on me, to the point that Bobby felt like an intruder, got up, threw on some clothes, and left the room. So there I was in the middle of steamy sex with this hot, passionate guy who only had eyes for me, at that particular moment in time. I still can't believe I did this, but I put on the brakes. Doug protested strongly, but I made him stop. Really. As much as I missed that dick of his, I knew my relationship was more important. I sent Doug away. Then I dressed and headed down the hall to the kitchen where, luckily, Bobby was having a solitary nightcap. I asked him to come back to our room. He did. We never discussed Doug. We had rules. And there was no need to revisit our agreement.

Of all the angels (and others) we entertained that summer, the only one I ever saw again was the one I least wanted to see. Wouldn't you know I would run into Doug the next afternoon on Commercial Street! He was obviously just as eager as I was to put the encounter behind us. After quick eye-contact, we both pretended not to have seen the other. And that was the end of that.

The candy store aspect was great fun, but there were other, less harmless situations to follow. In fact, I began to feel that I had left the Candy Store and entered The School of Life. I wouldn't give up a single memory, even though there were some hairy times to come.

Chapter Five

(You Make Me Feel Like)
A Natural Woman

. . . Before the day I met you, life was so unkind.
But your love was the key to my peace of mind
"Cause you make me feel,
You make me feel,
You make me feel like a natural woman.

Written by Carole King and Gerry Goffin, inspired by Atlantic Records producer Jerry Wexler, introduced by Aretha Franklin in 1967

"Isn't it amazing how sometimes having an enormous dick up one's ass can make one see the face of God? You wouldn't think the eyes and the ass were so closely attuned, would you? But they are!" I loved Bunny's act. It always made me laugh, even the third and fourth times I heard it.

As we settled into our work routine, I started to take an interest in the local food scene—Yankee seafood and Portuguese specialties in equal measure. I had always cooked. Hell, I baked my first cake at age five (with a little help from Betty Crocker). The few years I waited tables, in Chicago mostly, it was always the kitchen that fascinated me, not the dining room. And yet I thought I would become an actor or a director, and so I was never tempted to go to culinary school or try to get an entry-level kitchen job somewhere.

The term "foodie" had not been coined yet. That wouldn't appear until the early '80s in London. But I was certainly pouring myself into that mold, and Provincetown was a charming place to flow. On quiet afternoons I would poke around town, ask questions, and plan trips to various restaurants. The word slowly spread that I had a foodie bent, and gradually people would volunteer bits of food lore.

One evening in our second week, after Bunny's show as we were settling the checks, Anita said to me, "Sunny, why don't you come by the house tomorrow afternoon? I have some recipes from my mother-in-law you might be interested in, and maybe you could help me eat some of the *Pastéis de Nata* I baked—that Moises and I are not supposed to eat."

"Sure, what time?" was my enthusiastic reply.

"2:00?"

"Perfect! Thank you."

I had never been invited to a local home. Indeed, I had rarely been off Commercial Street. So, I was keen to see more of P'town from a local perspective. And I was growing really fond of Anita.

 📖

Anita and Moises lived in a neat house on a low hill not far from the Pilgrim Monument. When Anita greeted me at the door that early June afternoon and invited me in, I felt instantly welcome. The living room was comfy, with serviceable old upholstered furniture and charming watercolors on the walls, mostly local seascapes, painted by Anita herself, I learned. I had heard that Anita and Moises had a son named Paul who had died some years before. I looked about for some evidence of his memory. But we only just paused in the front room on our way to the kitchen, the obvious heart of the house.

Anita's kitchen was large, at least as large as the living room. It contained all the usual equipment—a big old gas range, a double porcelain sink nice and deep, a large white refrigerator as rounded as a pillow, lots of cabinets and drawers, a small wall of kitchen gadgets, and a small shelf of cookbooks. All the doorways and moldings were framed with pretty blue-and-white tiles. The center of the room, literally and figuratively, was a big pine table that served as a work station and Command Central for the Lopes family.

Anita sat me down, produced some beautiful little custard tarts—"My mother-in-law's recipe"—and poured me a small glass of amber richness. "This is a Bual," she told me. "Very sweet, but full of flavor." Indeed, it was. And it was wonderful with the pastry, which was rich with an overdose of egg yolks but restrained in the sugar department. As I helped myself to a second *pastel de nata*, I was mindful of how pretty it was—all golden brown from the heat of the oven that transforms lowly kitchen staples into silken luxuries.

"You know, we always had Madeira in the house when I was growing up. Never Port or Sherry," Anita said. I guess I looked blank, because she asked me, "Do you know why,

Sunny?" When I confessed to being clueless, she explained patiently, as if to a small child, "Because during the Revolution, the British could prevent wine shipments from reaching the Colonies from Porto and from Cadiz, where Sherry is shipped. But they couldn't manage to blockade the Madeira Islands. So, Madeira got through, and later it became a matter of national pride to drink Madeira instead of the others. My Yankee family never forgot that."

So much to learn, I thought.

"Do you know about Green Soup?" Anita asked.

I confessed that while I had eaten it—and liked it—in a restaurant in Provincetown, I didn't really know anything about it.

"It is usually considered to be the Portuguese national dish. If there is such a thing. Most people agree that all you do is cook some chopped onions and crumbled *linguiça* or *chouriço* sausage in a little olive oil, add diced potatoes and water to cover, simmer until the potatoes are tender, mash it up a bit so the potatoes get a little creamy, and then stir in the shredded greens just before serving. In Portugal they use collards, but we grow mostly kale around here. Kale is good, but it is hard to get it sliced fine enough, so you have to cook it a little longer. Joan at the greenmarket calls me whenever she gets in some collards. I rush over and get a big bunch. I can roll up the leaves and slice them as thin as hay, just the way they do in Portugal and Brazil. With shredded collards, you stir them in and the soup is ready to eat as soon as it comes back to the boil. That really is the best *Caldo Verde*. Have you been to the greenmarket? I'll take you by and introduce you to Joan.

She's a nice lady. And she has a really cute son, too."

"Anita, how did you get to Provincetown? You're from near Boston, aren't you?" I asked.

"Yes, from Quincy. When I was nineteen, my mother arranged for me to go with my aunt Wilma, who was the bohemian in the Winthrop family. She used to take a cottage for the summer in Provincetown. She would sketch all day and paint half the night. I had my time pretty much to myself, al-though Aunt Wilma was a stickler for cocktail hour and dinner together. So that summer, I fell in love first with Provincetown and then with a young man who was so beautiful I thought I would melt or turn to stone or something if I looked at him too long.

"That was Moises Lopes. We passed each other on Commercial Street a few times in early June, and then he stopped me one day and introduced himself, and offered to buy me a coffee. I accepted. We had a nervous "first date" as we both tried to figure out how to break the ice and breach the divide. But you know, nervous as I was, his steadiness gave me confidence, I guess. And I was able to open my heart to this young man who even a week before had seemed like a vision. You know, he looked tall, though he was under six feet. He carried himself like a bigger man. Still does. His hair was black and wavy, and his nose in profile was so straight and grand, like a monument. As far as I was concerned, he looked like a marble Greek god, only better. Because there was a warmth that radiated from him—still does—that made me feel surrounded by him, safe, protected. I felt so proud that he could love me!

"Moises is the son of a shipbuilder who had done pretty

well for himself and wanted his son to carry on the business. Moises was very responsible and dutiful—still is—and so there was no question that he would work in the family business. His only holdout was insisting on marrying me. Little Miss Winthrop. A Yankee girl. An Episcopalian! The family was not happy about it. Nor was mine. But everyone had to get over it.

"The short version of the story is, we got married and we took a bungalow on the edge of town, and started figuring out what married life is supposed to be. Moises went to work every day, and I cooked and cleaned and got pregnant right away. I loved it, actually, being pregnant. Some women do. It's not for everyone! The delivery was maybe the happiest day of my life.

"You know, Paul looked so much like Moises it was uncanny. And there I was with two of these dark beauties, the big one who fell in love with me, and the tiny one our love had produced. I was a very happy woman.

"Now, Sunny, get out of here and let me start dinner!"

I quickly said my thank-yous, and headed out into the afternoon sun. I was flushed with Madeira and the experience of having been invited into another's life, in equal measure, I think. The wind picked up and it was refreshing on my face. As I headed back to the hotel, I wondered how Bobby's and my love would bear fruit, as Anita's and Moises' had. Could I do it? Could I make the long haul? Was I strong enough? Was I worthy?

Chapter Six

Do You Want to Dance?

Do you wanna dance, and hold my hand?
Tell me you're my lover man.
Oh baby, do you wanna dance?

Written by Bobby Freeman, recorded by Freeman, The Beach Boys, Bette Midler, et al.

"Fucking is like eating a lobster—you have to put in a bit of effort to get to the really choice parts." Bunny was at it again. I loved his riffs on Fucking Is Like. . . . He had dozens of them.

"Fucking is like praying: it requires faith in the rightness of the moment.

"Fucking is like politics: no one wants to back a loser.

"Fucking is like cooking: quality in, quality out.

"Fucking is like driving a car: sometimes we don't even know why, we just need to go for a ride.

"Fucking is like carpentry: no power tool can equal a hand-rubbed finish.

"Fucking is like shopping: you can spot the right fit at twenty paces.

"Fucking is like a haircut: a hot guy with skilled hands can do wonders.

"Fucking is like a good night's sleep: it restores your faith in mankind.

"Fucking is like waking up in the morning: proof of life.

"Fucking is like a beautiful man who stops to say hello: proof of heaven."

I loved working Bunny's show. It was always great fun, and it meant that I was off work by 9:30.

One evening the second week in June when I had the late shift off, Bobby and I decided to go out exploring the famous Provincetown night life. We started with drinks at Atlantic House, a time-honored stop on any bar-crawl. It was great fun to be out with so many hot guys, but the bar was really crowded, and soon it began to feel a bit claustrophobic. It was a lovely night, so we headed farther west on Commercial Street to the Boatslip for its open-air bar.

We were able to grab one stool at the bar, overlooking the ongoing dance party around the pool. I insisted that Bobby sit and stake our claim. We ordered drinks. The full moon shone down on us like, like a full moon, actually. There really is no language to improve on the concept of moonlight. Silvery, yes. But even my favorite William Spratling bracelet—and it is a breathtaking accomplishment of the silversmith's art—pales in comparison to *La Luna* herself.

Now, lest you think that Debussy is the only musician to capture moonlight, I should tell you that Bobby did it too. I was sitting in an audience once when the chanteuse crooned about the moon shining down on some little town and what happened with each beam. And in support of her lament, Bobby provided moonbeams. I swear they were musical moonbeams, and they flowed right out of the keyboard. It was mesmerizing.

But that particular moonlit night, the very cute bartender— aren't they all, thank God—brought us our drinks. "What a beautiful evening," Bobby said. "Playing Jan's show is really tiring, but I'm glad we decided to get out tonight."

"So am I," I said.

And then someone touched my right shoulder and said, "Hi, I'm John. Wanna dance?" I turned to see a guy in a bright red T-shirt who was about my height, mid-20s, trim, with dark hair and eyes and a slightly Latin look. He also had a great smile and a really kissy mouth.

"Sure," I replied. Bobby didn't dance and I did, so my opportunities for dancing were limited. "Hold my drink?" I asked Bobby, for form's sake.

"Of course," he replied, and my new dance partner and I headed out into the crowd. The music was loud and the beat was visceral. It was a great feeling to let go and just dance, just be there on the dance floor, just be part of the pulsing rhythm and the twinkling lights and the sea of gyrating, sweating bodies. Mostly we danced separately, in '70s disco style. But John would also touch me at times, and pull me closer to him or

41

bump my body with his.

When we got close I was aware that John smelled great. Only later could I put a name to that scent, when it occurred to me that he smelled *exactly* like making love in moonlight, which of course was sort of what we were sort of doing. But in the middle of it all, it just smelled like summer on steroids. And it was entirely therapeutic. I hadn't realized how the vibe at the club with the J's had made me tense until dancing with John cleared away that tension. It had been a while since I had felt so free.

After a few songs, we walked over to the railing designed to keep people from falling into the Bay, and introduced ourselves more properly. I learned that his name was John Alegria, and that he was a native. John said, "Oh, you're at the Pilgrim House! You know, I worked there two summers. I was one of the Five Js. A charter member. Then last year I decided to take a summer course, so Jake replaced me. Have you met Jake yet, Jake Holman?"

Had I met him? I had already lost more sleep over Jake than I cared to admit. But what would cause John to bring up the subject? "Yes, I met Jake, but why do you ask?"

"Only that Jake has a way of putting himself in the middle of things. Just thought you should know."

I pursued the topic briefly, but John seemed ready to drop it. So instead of talking we danced again. Then we headed back to the bar. *No fucking way!* I thought. But sure enough, there was Jake Holman standing next to Bobby's barstool, pressed in close against his leg, laughing and talking in Bobby's ear.

"Speak of the devil! Hi, Jake. We were just talking about

you," John said. "How've you been?" John and Jake embraced and exchanged a few pleasantries while I tried to control the agitation in my gut that Jake's sudden appearance had brought on. *Yes, he's a hot little thing, but so is Charles Manson,* I thought. And then I thought, *He may have a really nice butt, but so what?* And then I thought, *This is ridiculous. Bobby is mine, isn't he?* And then I thought, *There's no such thing as mine, is there?* And then I thought, *Hot little guys are a-dime-a-dozen.* And then I thought, *Hot little guys who are also musical and maybe even talented are perhaps a rarer breed.* And then I decided to stop thinking.

After a few awful minutes, I turned to Bobby and said, "It's getting kind of late, Sweetie. Maybe we should head home."

"You're absolutely right," Bobby responded. "We adults need to set a good example."

"I'm so glad we met!" John said.

"See you around the quad," Jake said.

"Fuck you very much," I did *not* say, of course, as much as I wanted to. Instead I said, "Good night, all!"

I gave John a quick hug while Jake was giving Bobby a long hug, and then we switched partners, briefly. Jake actually embraced me, quickly, with more challenge than affection in his hug. But there was also something in Jake's embrace, cursory as it was, that stirred up things down in my crotch region. Even though his attention was certainly not focused on me, he still managed to get a rise out of me, as he always seemed to do, one way or another.

Walking back to the hotel, our ears abuzz with the aftereffect of loud music, Bobby and I were silent as we drank in the scene—the unfiltered moonlight, the wind-down of another

Provincetown night, the singles at the "meat-rack" in front of City Hall hoping to get lucky. I couldn't help but muse on how life works, how a moment of abandon is followed by a jab of fear like a punch below the belt. *Why does everything have to be so fucking hard?* I wondered. I couldn't have known that the universe was just warming up.

Chapter Seven

What a Difference a Day Makes

. . . Lord, what a difference a day makes,
There's a rainbow before me.
Skies above can't be stormy,
Since that moment of bliss,
That thrilling kiss.

It's heaven when you
Find romance on your menu,
What a difference a day made,
And the difference is you.

Written by Maria Grever, English lyrics by Stanley Adams, popularized
by Dinah Washington in 1959

Jan was "on" that next morning when we were having coffee in the kitchen. "You know, Dinah Washington was a buddy of mine. She used to give me wonderful dresses, and wigs, too. One day I was at her apartment and we were trying on things, and then she suddenly said, 'What time is it, Pussy?' She called me Pussy.

45

"So, I said, 'It's noon.'

" 'Shit, Pussy. Grab your coat!' So, we went flying out of her building and into a taxi. After a rough trip through midtown traffic, we arrived at a recording studio, where an arranger, a conductor, two technicians, and twenty-three studio musicians were waiting in stony silence. I don't even know how many hours late she was. Dinah burst into the studio, strutted up to the microphone, threw her mink coat on the floor behind her, and said, 'Let's get this shit done! Don't waste my time!' And that was *What a Difference a Day Makes*. In one take!"

Actually, I loved Jan's stories. And I always suspected they were spot-on accurate, too. He had enough fantasy in his life on stage every night. The rest of the time he seemed to live in the reality space. It occurred to me that Bobby and I should make a difference with that very day, so I said to him, "Let's head out and wander around town. I haven't seen that much of it yet."

"Good idea," Bobby said, "as long as you don't want to rent a bicycle. I don't cycle."

"Oh, don't be silly," I replied. "Everyone can ride a bicycle."

"Well, now you know someone who can't." Bobby was firm, so I let it go. So much to learn.

"I'm just going to put on some sandals. Are you ready to go out?" I asked.

"Sure. Just give me five minutes," he said.

We headed out onto Commercial Street a few minutes later, turning left, for a change. It was a perfect summer day. The morning haze had all burned off, and the sun was brilliant except for an occasional pass behind a big, puffy cloud. The slight breeze off the bay kept things feeling fresh. I was a very happy boy.

As we waved to the nice old gay couple that owned Poor Richard's Buttery, I wondered what exactly felt so compelling about Provincetown. Other New England fishing villages have quaint clapboard shops and houses. There are galleries and restaurants and antique stores many places. But there was something so easy and inviting about P'town.

I didn't know much about it at the time, but I've done my homework since. Provincetown attracted a wonderful variety of people, then as now. We smart young gay boys felt that it was ours, of course, when, in reality, it also belonged to other tourists, beachgoers, families, day-trippers from Boston, and other types from the Northeast. But especially, Provincetown belongs to its citizens. They are a hardy lot, for the most part. Some are crusty old Yankees whose families have lived—and fished—there for generations. After all, the Mayflower was anchored in the harbor while the Pilgrims sorted out a location for their new colony.

And speaking of fish, there was a Portuguese migration to P'town and surrounding towns and states that started in colonial times, really took off in the 1870s, and continued briskly up until the 1990s or so, spurred by political dangers, poverty, lack of opportunity, and natural disasters back home. Fishing, whaling, and textile factory work were the draws, as well as the promise of a new life in the land of the free.

And then there are the artsy people. They began to set up

studios and galleries in P'town as early as the turn of the twentieth Century. 1916 was the year that all the arts—and the gay population—got a boost with the founding of the Provincetown Theatre. Think Eugene O'Neill and a new brand of American drama. So, artsy has been around for a century, with the gay invasion as an economic force building to full strength during the 1960s.

What a brew! But on that lovely June afternoon, I knew only that I felt very welcome in this town that had taken me in for the whole summer. The politics at the Madeira Room was less welcoming, but that particular afternoon was proving to be delightfully J-free.

After a half-mile or so, Bobby and I worked our way back on the bay side of Commercial Street, and discovered even more shops and galleries. Just as we passed Pilgrim House, I was pleased to see John Alegria headed in our direction. We greeted him, and he said, "I'm just going to my cousin's house to take her this birthday cake my mother baked. I won't be more than fifteen minutes. Do you like oysters?" he asked.

"Love them!" Bobby and I replied in unison.

"Then we should go out for oysters," John said. "My father knows the best oysterman in Wellfleet. The water stays cold enough through the end of June so the oysters are still really meaty and good. Well, they're always good, but they're even better from cold water. So let's go eat some."

"In Wellfleet?" I asked.

"Well, we could go to *Ye Olde Oyfter Houfe* some time if you like, but let's stay in town. We can meet at the Old Reliable. Dad delivers to them every day. Do you guys have any time off?"

I looked at Bobby and he seemed enthusiastic, so I said, "We both start about 6:30 tonight, but we're free until then."

"Then meet me at 2:30, and we'll make an afternoon of it."

"Perfect," Bobby said. And John was off on his errand.

Getting out and about was making me very happy. The idea of spending time with John also seemed to make me very happy. A different thing. I knew it, too. But I hoped it was all harmless, and decided to leave it at that. Window shopping and dawdling, we worked our way slowly a few blocks farther west on Commercial Street. And then we were there, at the little pier on the Bay attached to Old Reliable Fish House, and right on time.

Resort towns have a different clock from other cities. The hours between lunch and cocktails might be quiet some places, but the Old Reliable was humming with life and libations. John had arrived a minute before and gotten us a table near the bar. We settled in. "See that big glass cask under the bar? The owner imports his wines from Portugal in those casks and then hooks them up to a siphon. The white is a little rough, but it's really nice with oysters," John said.

Indeed, it was. The oysters arrived, a dozen at a time, so fresh I could have sworn that some of them were quivering. They were plump and delicious, with that extraordinary flavor profile that is really impossible to do justice with words—sweet and saline in equal measure with just enough minerality to create a little zing on the palate. How many dozens could one down and still want more? I have yet to test the full possibilities, but that particular afternoon I managed two dozen, anyway. Bobby ate even more.

I didn't know anything about Old Reliable at the time, and had never heard of Chef Howard Mitcham and his no-nonsense seafood and Portuguese cooking. We made up for that later. But our oyster afternoon was such fun, I will always remember the sheer pleasure of it—the restaurant humming with happiness, the drafts of coarse young wine, the plates of sparkling oysters, and John with his wonderful smile and generous ease. I thought, *This is truly* **A Day Well Spent** (the play that inspired *The Matchmaker* and *Hello, Dolly*). And, mercifully, John was the only J in sight.

Chapter Eight

Falling in Love Again

Falling in love again.
Never wanted to.
What am I to do?
I can't help it.

Love's always been my game
Play it how I may.
I was made that way.
I can't help it.

Written by Friedrich Hollaender, English lyrics by Sammy Lerner, introduced by Marlene Dietrich in 1934

"Falling in love again, never vanted to" came a throaty voice from the little stage. The comic Kraut accent, the sucked-in cheeks, the darting eyes belonged to Jan Cooper. His Marlene Dietrich was deliciously tough and grand, nearly immobile in tight sequined chiffon fashioned after the gown that the lady herself was wearing for her stage appearances that decade. Seating himself carefully on the piano, Jan crossed his legs dramatically, and then observed, "Dat bwought a tear to youw eye, ya? Ya, I shtill got it. De only ting is, I've 'ad it so long, no vone else vants it!" Ba-dum-pum.

It may seem a strange category of entertainment today, drag impressions of famous celebrities. Did it come out of German cabaret, or English Music Hall, or who knows? It was popular in the US from the '40s on, but once the grandes dames of the genre began to die out—in the mid- '80s—there was not really a new crop to replace them. I only know of one guy who is still plying the craft in P'town to this day. But that summer there was a bumper crop. In fact, they were all there.

Drag was only one aspect of these shows, helmed by men who did stand-up impressions. They had to look interesting, sing a little, maybe dance a little. Some were okay with the term Drag Queen, but most preferred to be called something else—female impersonators, or sometimes, female impressionists. But that can be confusing, because the category Female Impressionists includes Mary Cassatt, so it's not the same thing.

We thought of Jan as the queen of P'town, because we knew him and were working for him. But there were others that summer. In fact, all of the major American drag players (and a Canadian one, too) were there, working the whole summer or stopping in for a concert or two, just to keep an oar in. There was also a sassy female singer whose larger-than-life characters were so outlandish they might as well have been drag. And we met them all.

The Monday of our third week, Bobby said, "Why don't we go out and catch some of the competition? They all have matinées, so we can manage it. What about starting tomorrow afternoon"

"Sure," I said. "Sounds like fun."

That night, after Jan's show, Bobby came over to the bar to hang out for a few minutes. And Jake walked in, to say hello to the other Js—which he did with alarming frequency. I was always aware of Jake when he was in the house. I felt his presence even from across the room. I wondered if it was something I could smell, so keen was my perception of him. And John's warning was fresh in my mind, so Jake's presence was becoming increasingly alarming.

"Hi, Bobby," Jake said. "What have you guys been up to?"

"Not much, but tomorrow afternoon we're going to see some drag shows."

"May I tag along?" Jake asked.

"Of course," Bobby said. "Meet us at the Boatslip at 1:00."

And so it was all arranged, and so I began to feel even more vertiginous than usual. *Shit!* What are the chances of going away for the summer and finding a Bobby acolyte who is dying to get back to the vestry and out of his cassock, with Bobby! Well, call me paranoid, but I swear it happened. And I had not the slightest idea how to handle it.

"Vhat am I to do? I cahn't help it." Our first Dietrich of the day was a young Canadian named Charles Greer at The Boatslip. It was a fun show. Greer was a skilled impressionist, and he also had a sweetness about him, a vulnerable quality, that made his ladies almost poignant, even while the jokes were rip-roaring. I was more interested in keeping an eye on Jake, however. Before, during, and after the show.

Jake was so quick, so physical. He could suddenly punctuate a joke by pinching Bobby's left nipple, or nibbling his ear, or grabbing his crotch playfully—playfully for Jake, that is. I thought it anything but play. I thought it aggressive, and I was horrified. Actually, I was pretty much immobilized.

After Charles Greer's show, the three of us headed to a café for a sandwich and a glass of wine. I think the food and drink were pretty good, but my focus was elsewhere.

"I can't believe Roger Bryant is here," Bobby said, referring to our next Dietrich of the day. "I was taken to see that old queen in Hollywood in the '50s. You know, Bette Davis always said that he was the only one who could "do" her." Bryant was a fixture at the Crown & Anchor for twenty years. He performed an early show that would give me time for about half of it before I had to get back and set up for Bunny's 5:00 show at the Madeira Room. Our little band—two-thirds of it merry—headed for the Crown & Anchor showroom.

"Men cluster to me like moths around a flame. And if der vings burn, you know I'm not to blame." **This** Marlene Dietrich was Roger Bryant. How can I explain Roger Bryant to you? He was the elder stateswoman of the genre, for sure. If you sat me down under harsh interrogation lights and threatened to pull out my fingernails, I doubt I could give you a cleaner description of what this man did on stage than what I am trying to offer now. He was a big man, tall, and paunchy. He was about sixty at the time. The other impersonator/impressionists had wigs and costumes that at least gave the illusion of glamour and glitz. Bryant used mostly his own rather scary face.

Tallulah Bankhead was a particular pride of his. Jan Cooper no longer "did" Bankhead because he adjusted his act to remove stars who had died. I thought he had the right idea. Roger Bryant, however, was still doing his 1950 act. "Hello, Dahling!"

Scary as he was, Roger Bryant was the least of my fears that balmy June afternoon as I left the Crown & Anchor in the middle of the show and headed back to the hotel. Jake had flustered me to the point that I couldn't quite tell what was what. *Is Bobby falling for this guy? Is he more attractive than I am? Well, that's a given, but is my life falling apart right in front of my face?* All of this, and more, I asked myself as I stumbled back to the hotel and put on my work outfit—black slacks, white shirt, and a little bow-tie.

Down in the Madeira Room I began to set up the tables in my station and pretend that nothing was wrong. Bunny didn't miss much, however, so as he arrived and headed to the dressing room to begin the transformation from mere mortal to diva, he stopped at the table where I was polishing glasses. Bunny took me by the chin with one of his large, expressive hands, and said, "Miss Saltine, you look like shit!"

"Sounds about right," I answered.

"Come by my place tomorrow afternoon, about 1:00, and

tell your old Aunt Bunny all about it."

I thanked him for the invitation, and started to feel a bit better. The reality of work pushed the terror to the back of my brain, for the next few hours, at least. By the time I got back to the room that night I was almost myself again. I said nothing to Bobby about Jake. I had no idea what to say, or what to think, for that matter.

"So how was the rest of Roger Bryant's act?" I asked in my best approximation of chirpy banter.

"About the same, I'm afraid," was Bobby's reply.

We were both tired, so we went right to bed. Bobby fell into rhythmic breathing almost as soon as his head hit the slightly lumpy pillow. I was not so lucky. Another Scotch helped a little, but my brain kept replaying the day and a whole host of negative events from various times in my life. *What the hell is going on?* I wondered over and over.

"Love's alvays been my game, play it how I may. I vaz made dat vay! I cahn't help it." I felt that I had had enough Marlene Dietrich to last a lifetime, but the record kept playing in my head. Eventually sleep claimed me, and I was still deep in it when the alarm went off the next morning at 11:00.

I got out of bed, feeling even worse than I looked, and threw on shorts and a T. Heading to the kitchen to make coffee for Bobby and me, I wondered, *What the hell will today bring?*

"What are you up to today, Sunshine?" Bobby asked me, as we sipped the very good coffee I had discovered at a funny little food shop that catered to locals.

"Bunny asked me to stop by this afternoon," I replied.

"How nice! Say hello for me."

"Of course. And what about you?" I asked, not really wanting to hear the answer.

"I'm going to take the afternoon off and go lie on the beach with Randy and Jake," Bobby answered.

"Don't get burned," I said, without really knowing whether I was talking about sun-burn prevention or some danger to the heart.

Chapter Nine

Sweet and Lowdown

If you need a tonic
And the need is chronic,
If you're in a crisis,
My advice is:

Grab a cab and go down
To where the band is playing,
Where milk and honey flow down,
And everybody's saying,
"Blow that sweet and lowdown!"

Lyrics by Ira Gershwin, music by George Gershwin, from the musical
Tip-Toes, 1925

Bunny Babbit seemed mysterious to me. Unabashedly
"out there" on stage, the public Bunny was brash and loud.
The private Bunny was free, easy, and affectionate with his
friends. But his past and his romantic life were locked away in
the bank vault of his heart, not to be shared with the likes of
me. I think he grew up in Alabama, but that was only hearsay.

Once when I started to ask him a question about his childhood, he clapped a lid on the subject immediately, and I knew better than to try and pry it open.

Bunny's little apartment behind a guest house was, well, quite something. Bobby would have called the decor "early modern whorehouse." Scarves on the sconces, fans everywhere, too many readings of Tennessee Williams. Blanche DuBois after shopping at Pier 1. Lots of pink and fuchsia. Invisible clouds of floral essence. Bunny held court from a rattan peacock chair and served tea on a small table held up by carved elephants. Except it wasn't tea he served but mysterious beverages that were always colorful, intensely sweet, and deadly strong.

"So, tell me all about it, little boy," Bunny said after I had taken a large swig of the potion, and it had begun to work its almost-immediate magic.

"Oh, I don't know, Bunny. It's probably nothing," I replied.

"'Nothing' looks quite different from what I see on your face," he said.

I took a deep breath and then let out a sort of general recap of the previous day's events and my feelings of hopelessness about them. "Maybe I'm not making Bobby happy. Maybe he should be with someone who has more his tastes, someone who has more in common. "

"Wow, what a crock of shit! You're not telling me what's going on," Bunny replied.

"There's this guy who hangs around the hotel. His name is Jake. . . "

"You mean Jake Holman? That little weasel has the right name, all right. *Holman!* Huh! He will eat up your *whole man*, given half a chance! Miss Saltine, are you just plain stupid, or have you been struck blind and dumb, too? 'Cause it looks like you are fixing to have your future fall apart while you sit here sipping Singapore Slings with your old Aunt Bunny."

"But Bunny, I couldn't stand in Bobby's way. I just want him to be happy!"

"Now you listen here, Caldonia. And you let this penetrate that hard head of yours." Bunny was almost menacing. "You have a quality man there. And whether you deserve him or not is beside the point. He wants you! Now, where is he?"

"He's at the beach. Sunbathing. With Jake," I answered.

"So you are going to go to the beach, and get Bobby, and drag him back to the hotel, where you will give him the best blowjob of your sorry not-so-young life!"

I knew that Bunny was right about the sex part, crude as it seemed. Pleasing your man, maintaining relationships. I got all of that. Given all the stupid things I have done, still, in all, I am not a stupid person. I marshaled my forces and headed out for battle.

Arriving at the bay beach practically across the street from the Pilgrim House, I got a sinking feeling as I spied Randy stretched out on his sand chair sunning himself—alone. "Oh, Bobby left—with Jake," Randy told me, looking up from his pulp novel, glancing over the rim of his sunglasses with a theatrical "Uh huh!"

I knew that I should head back to the hotel. It was only natural to fight for my mate, to guard my territory. But it was as if paralysis had set in. I couldn't seem to budge from that little spit of sand right off Commercial Street. When my limbs were functional again, I said a lame goodbye to Randy and wandered off, avoiding the hotel for fear I might glimpse the unthinkable—the love-of-my-life in the arms of a greedy little home-wrecker. Instead, I found my way to the Crown & Anchor, carefully avoiding the show room, walking through the courtyard to the open-air bar on the way to the pool. It was only about three in the afternoon, so things were fairly quiet. No tea-dance crowd yet. I found a bit of empty real estate where I perched myself and ordered a double vodka on-the-rocks. As I sipped it and gradual waves of calm began to flow over me, I tried to sort out the situation.

So what am I going to do about this mess? If indeed there really is a mess. How do I find out? What if I force a confrontation and Bobby has to make a choice? What if he chooses Jake over me? After an hour or so of fruitless cogitation, I left the bar and slowly made my way back down Commercial Street to the hotel.

Bobby was sitting at the little desk, a half-finished music chart in front of him. He sat on a towel, to keep his naked body from resting directly on the funny old chair. He had just showered, by the look of his wet hair and clean skin. Too clean, in my opinion, as if in an attempt to remove evidence. I looked around—and sniffed around—for evidence of Jake.

Looking up as I walked in, Bobby said, "Hi, Sunshine. How is Bunny?"

"Oh, you know. He's Bunny," I answered weakly.

"You look a little the worse for demon rum. Better grab a quick lie-down before work. I have to finish charting this arrangement, but I'll be very quiet. Just stretch out for a half hour. I'll wake you in time."

Obediently, I lay down right on the bedspread without removing anything but my shoes. But even in my weakened condition, I had the good sense to unwrap my pillow from the bedspread, in the interest of avoiding chenille marks on my cheek. Not pretty. And so, I conked out for a half-hour of deep, mercifully dreamless sleep. When Bobby awakened me, with a kiss, consciousness gradually seeped back in. I felt like shit, but I hoped a shower would help. It did. I dressed and headed down to the Madeira Room as if nothing had happened. And, perhaps, nothing had. But how could I know?

Chapter Ten

Bewitched

. . . I'm wild again,
Beguiled again,
A whimpering, simpering child again.
Bewitched, bothered, and bewildered am I. . .

Written by Lorenz Hart and Richard Rodgers, introduced by Vivienne
Segal in the musical *Pal Joey*, 1940

We used to see Heath Woodford around the hotel often
during the day. As handyman for an aging building in a rather
harsh climate, he was sure to find something that needed his
skill to set it right. Heath was very quiet, but he had a ready
smile and exceptionally pretty, even white teeth with a tiny
chip on the inside edge of the right front one. Occasionally he
would join us for a drink on the little porch on the second
floor in the back, where the warm rays of late afternoon sunlight—coming in as they do almost level with the horizon—
would set fire to his golden-brown eyes, making them appear
as if they were tiger-eye that had mysteriously come alive.

Heath was not exactly what you could call a red head—

certainly not a carrot-top. But there was an appealing ginger quality to his hair and trim beard that set off his fair skin to good advantage. There he was a denizen of the beach— summers in P'town and the rest of the year at home in Halifax, Nova Scotia—and yet when I remember him he is hardly sun-kissed. In memory, Heath is almost pale, with a delicate network of blue veining just slightly visible beneath the surface of his translucent skin.

I have had a fantasy through the years, maybe it was even a dream, where Heath and I are lying together on a sofa in the afternoon sunlight, and I am so close to him that I can not only share his sweet breath and feel his heartbeat against my chest, but I can see a tiny blue vein in his temple that pulses in rhythm with that heartbeat. And that pulse and my proximity to it are so intimate, so fragile, that I feel I am privy to a wonder of nature, like the birth of a fawn or something. And I daren't move or even exhale too violently for fear that the moment will evaporate, that it will not only end but disappear into unreality.

The fantasy Heath was a glorious creature, but the real-life Heath was also a pleasure to see and know. He had a sturdy quality. Not like a lumberjack. More like the yeoman-farmer that anyone would be glad to lie down for, and be proud to bear his child. You might have been tempted to put a helmet with a nose guard on him and cast him as one of King Richard's archers. He certainly had a wonderful nose, worth guarding. But in my fantasy film Heath will always be Robin Hood.

One afternoon the third week in June I was in the group

shower across from our room—not exactly a gang shower, two showerheads only—when Heath walked in with a light apology for needing to use our bathroom because the plumbing in his was out of whack. New parts ordered, delivery not until tomorrow, that sort of thing. I couldn't have been less offended. In fact, I was so thrilled that it took every bit of my self-training in composure to pretend that his naked presence was of no interest. It gave new meaning to feigned indifference and stolen glances. Gay boys learn all of this at an early age, if they are to survive in a society that abhors them. But my technique was getting a real workout. Heath, on the other hand, seemed genuinely without the slightest interest in me beyond a hint of embarrassment at having intruded.

There he stood—or rather lathered and rinsed—in all his simple masculinity. His body was lean and tightly muscled, strong but not overgrown. He was, in short, exactly what he needed to be and nothing more. Mind, body, and spirit converged into a harmonious whole that left me breathless. He was generously hung, but not scary. Again, there was balance and appropriateness in his dimensions as well as his demeanor. His balls hung just low enough to be visible as tempting, individual ripe fruits begging to be plucked. But you know better than to get me started on balls. I couldn't really see the delicate blue veining that surely webbed his whole pubic package, but I knew it was there, just below the pretty tuft of gingery hair that trailed up his flat belly in a narrow pathway to his navel.

Heath's ass was also just what it should be: strong, balanced, with those wonderful dips on both sides like sculpted indentations made for grabbing with the palms. I was flooded with an urge to drop down there, seize those dips like handles, and bury my face between Heath's legs. Funny thing about men's butts: it is as if God looked at the Adam he had sculpted, and just before breathing into him the breath of life, God couldn't resist giving that beautiful butt a little pinch. Eve was to get that pinch too, of course, but Adam had the original model.

This shower memory has a considerable amount of fantasy in it, I grant you. One of those cherished Heath fantasies has me gently peeling back his ample foreskin to reveal a beautiful dickhead of the most delicate shade of coral pink, like the pearly inside of one of those over-sized white conch shells from the tropics and '50s motels in Florida. It seems that only gingers can have a glans of that shade, and only gingers can have crotch colors that seem to clash. Pink and auburn. Odd. But compelling, nevertheless.

I never went there, of course. Had I done so—not that my intrusion on his lack of privacy would have been welcome—I might never have made it back to reality. I might have dived into the warmth of his crotch, soap and all, and stayed there, taking him into my mouth, up my ass, wherever I could get him. I might have clung to him with desperate longing, hoping to consume him, hoping he would consume me, hoping to fuse. I might have gone crazy, or at least to another realm. I might have chucked my whole life in a wild attempt to follow some fantasy. I might have changed everything.

But I did not change everything. Nor did I have any real desire to. When I got out of that shower, dried off, and walked back across the hall to Bobby's and my room, I was pretty much the same boy who had just left it. It was, I guess, a bit like losing one's virginity: It feels that it should be a transformative experience, but unless the unlucky former virgin lives in some ultra-orthodox society that stones sexual transgressors, the experience of losing one's virginity passes all but unnoticed by the world. As much as nothing had happened and nothing had really changed, in fact my *heart* was changed in a tiny though fundamental way. It expanded to include a new space just large enough to house a small ache. And yet the new space was invisible from the outside, and my life proceeded as if that shower had never happened. Or so I thought at the time.

📖

"What do you know about Heath?" I asked Bunny the next afternoon as his place.

"Alright, Miss Saltine. You listen to your Auntie, now. Heath Woodford is a very nice man who has a very nice husband back home in Halifax, and that's that. No one is going to get anywhere with him—though thousands have tried—least of all a bit of fluff like you. You are twenty-six years old! Do you think quality husbands are waiting around every corner? Maybe for the great beauties. That's not you! You think that pretty little okra of yours, sweet as it may be, is going to land you another great catch? You have a fabulous man! So now why don't you go back to the hotel, grab him, and take care of business. Don't you fuck this up, Miss Saltine! If I hear that you are off making a fool of yourself it won't be pretty!"

Bunny's advice sobered me. A bit, at least.

Chapter Eleven

Always

I'll be loving you, Always,
With a love that's true, Always.

. . . Days may not be fair, Always.
That's when I'll be there, Always.
Not for just an hour,
Not for just a day,
Not for just a year,
But Always.

Written by Irving Berlin as a wedding gift for his fiancée Ellin McKay in 1925

"Fucking is like taking a shower: it cleanses the entire body." Bunny was deep into my favorite part of his show.

"Fucking is like taking a nap: it restores.

"Fucking is like putting on a new suit: it makes us feel beautiful.

"Fucking is like making soup: the better the ingredients, the richer the broth.

"Fucking is like blacksmithing: forging bonds is the same in all media.

"Fucking is like alchemy: even base metal looks golden in the right light.

"Fucking is like magic: in fact, it **is** magic.

"Fucking is like music: it don't mean a thing if it ain't got that swing.

"Fucking is like gardening: it helps little things grow.

"Fucking is like glass blowing: super-heated bodies must be handled with care.

"Fucking is like architecture: the beauty is in the function.

"Fucking is like a down comforter: it makes us feel all warm and cuddly.

"Fucking is like opera: it leaves you feeling that everything is possible."

That evening, not only did I get a welcome dose of Bunny, but also an invite from Anita. Which was even more precious.

Anita was in the middle of making beef stew when I arrived the next afternoon. "Paul's favorite," she told me. The kitchen was filled with warmth and the perfume of sautéing onions as she poured me a glass of Madeira. "This one is a Sercial," she told me. "Medium dry. Nice to sip, but I can cook with it, too."

So much to learn in this wide world. I drank in new experiences like the sponge I have always been. The wine was delicious, rich and slightly nutty, but definitely not sherry.

Anita seemed pleased that I was learning something, but she also shook her head slightly from time to time, as if my ignorance truly shocked her.

"Can I ask you about Paul?" I said.

"Yes, Sunny. I don't get to talk about him very often. Moises and I never go there. And friends and relatives know the story, so there isn't much to say these days."

"So what was he like?" I asked.

"Paul was a very sweet child. Some are, you know. Others are aggressive and peevish. I've seen little boys who are rough, even violent. But Paul was always a nice kid, generous, thoughtful. I also have to say that he got more handsome every day, if you can forgive that coming from his mother.

"Moises and I talked about having another child, but my doctor said it was not such a great idea. Something about my plumbing. You don't want to know. Moises was disappointed, but we were so happy with Paul that he filled our lives quite nicely.

"I guess I always knew that Paul was gay. At least I always knew that he was different from other boys. Gentle, loving. And funny, too. Moises didn't want to see it, so we never really talked about it until one day when Paul was seventeen. He developed a crush on a classmate, a real Yankee named Robert. This golden boy was not kind like Paul was. He sensed the attraction and made fun of it, made fun of Paul. The story got out, as these things always do. Before long it was all over town.

"Moises was horrified. Finally, I sat him down and said, 'Moises, our son is a wonderful young man. You know that.

73

Now, let's talk about his *heart*, not his *linguiça*, nice as it is (I imagine, considering the source).' Moises loved Paul so much that he eventually got over himself. And I think their relationship got better after that. Honesty is a powerful force, you may have noticed.

"After high-school, Paul started at the New England School of Art & Design. In Boston. He was in the BFA program. And then he came home summers and worked on a fishing boat. It was hard work, but he seemed to enjoy it. The physicality of it agreed with him, I think, and it was so different from his life in Boston. It made him feel balanced, I guess.

"After college, he decided to stay on with the fishing boat for a while. He hadn't decided exactly what to do next with his painting, but he wanted to keep busy. One morning in early October, five years ago, as the winch strained to haul in the catch, a cable snapped, whipped Paul in the face, and knocked him in the water. His boatmates scooped him out very quickly, but the cable had severed his carotid artery on the left side of his neck. So, Paul had nearly bled to death by the time they got him back on deck. Pressure compresses only just slowed the hemorrhaging a little. And there was nothing else that anyone could do. Within a few minutes he was gone."

We sat quietly for what seemed like a very long time. Tears streamed silently down Anita's cheeks. I was so moved that I could think of absolutely nothing to say. Eventually, it was Anita who broke the silence.

"The crew was so upset they took a few days off from fishing. All of them came by the house to express their sympathy, in threes and fours. I swear they all ended up in tears. Paul had been a part of so many lives. And his death seemed so senseless. Moises and I were both touched by the tributes, the black ribbons tied to the masts of fishing boats, the outpouring of support and affection from neighbors. But the funeral was a nightmare for me, with the whole fucking fleet in attendance, pardon my French. Everyone was able to walk in but my Paul, and he was the only one I really wanted there, the only one I wanted to see and talk with. I was numb for months. Years, actually.

"After Paul's death, I could never bring myself to go to the Blessing of the Fleet. It's coming up on Sunday afternoon. Bunny says it's time. Moises won't go, I'm sure. But Bunny is going to take me, and it will be fine."

"May I come along?" I asked.

"Of course. With Bunny on one arm and you on the other, what could go wrong?"

"You and Bunny seem unlikely friends, somehow," I said.

"Well, I admit I found him a bit shocking at first. But as I got to know him I accepted his humor and now I even look forward to hearing some of the grossest jokes over and over. But it was really after Paul's death that Bunny turned out to be such a kind friend, like a rock when my little world was teetering in the sand.

"Bunny reminded me to cherish the good, to let go of guilt, and to accept my new reality. I thought I was going to die, and I was afraid that maybe I wouldn't. Moises was so shattered that he disappeared behind this—macho mask. I was so alone. I don't think I could have gotten through it without

75

Bunny. I will always be grateful for that. And as far as I am concerned, he can do no wrong. But I never let him cook for me!"

Anita got up and went to a little kitchen drawer, the one where special things that defy classification end up. She carefully retrieved from the bottom of the drawer a small silver picture frame, hardly more than locket-sized. And she handed it to me. I held my breath as I looked, and of course there was Paul, a junior Moises but with his mother's sweetness around the mouth, and just as handsome as Anita had claimed. More handsome, really. I was speechless, again, making it how many times that day?

"Sunny, I want you to take that picture, and I want you to go home so I can get on with my day. Will you do that for me?"

I assured Anita that I could perform both of her requests, and I pulled myself together and left as soon as I could manage it. I walked back to the Pilgrim House in a bit of a daze. It took time for me to sort it all out. And the only thing that brings the memory into anything like sharp focus is that now, one of my most cherished possessions is a tiny photo of a beautiful young man I never would have met, except that his mother introduced him to me from the depths of her ample heart. And he haunts me to this day.

The Blessing of the Fleet is part of the Portuguese Day festivities on and around MacMillan Pier in the heart of town. It includes a procession of dignitaries—men in feathered cocked hats and uniforms, festival queens in elaborate gowns—plus marching bands and folk dancers. The Bishop and his entourage walked slowly in procession from the church to the pier. Bunny, Anita, and I had found a perch toward the center of the pier. Anita had carefully chosen to wear a red dress. Nothing that smacked of mourning would do for this occasion. Bunny and I had dressed up a bit, too, as one did in those days.

The Bishop's procession passed us and proceeded to the end of the pier. In place at a microphone, the Bishop intoned his litany in the kind of sing-song voice that always makes me tune out and think I am hearing just a bunch of mumbo-jumbo. There was incense rising to the heavens, and mournful bells tolled. Wreaths of flowers were offered to the waters of the Bay. Each boat that passed the Bishop's reviewing stand received a triple sprinkling of holy water. I assumed that one of those boats was the one that Paul died on, but I didn't dare ask which.

I like ceremonies. *Not so different from Venice marrying the sea,* I thought. Or maybe it was like a New Orleans funeral, with a jazz band in the procession to the cemetery. No, not a funeral, exactly, but more like a memorial service, where we are supposed to celebrate through our grief. And sometimes I find it hard to tell celebrations apart.

At last, all the boats had passed the Bishop and received their anointment—even the one that killed Paul, whichever one it was—and all the dances had been danced, and all the songs sung, and it was over. And then we went to eat. As

77

people do after ceremonies.

Portuguese food, of course. Anita had booked a table at her favorite restaurant for the three of us plus Moises. He was waiting when we arrived. We four settled in, ordered food, and drank wine. It turned out to be a really nice meal, and I was sorry that Bobby had decided not to join us. The green soup was not as good as what Anita had taught me to make, but it would do nicely.

Anita seemed relieved that the Blessing was over. Moises seemed relieved too, although it may have just been the wine. Bunny joked and laughed, and never mentioned the ceremony. He had told Anita it was time to get back into her life, she had taken his advice, and that was that. All of this I understood instinctively without explanation. I only wished I could figure out what was happening in *my* life.

Chapter Twelve

I Can Cook, Too

. . . I'm a man's ideal of a perfect meal
Right down to the demi-tasse.
I'm a pot of joy for a hungry boy,
Baby, I'm cookin' with gas.

. . . Oh, I'm a paté,
A marron glacé,
A dish you will wish you had took.
And what's more, Baby, I can cook!

Music and lyrics by Leonard Bernstein, introduced by Nancy Walker in
On the Town (book and other lyrics by Comden & Greene), 1944

The Fourth of July fell on a Sunday that year, perfect for
our picnic plans. We had it all organized. Two of John's
friends were coming from Boston, driving over in a Jeep.
John had his Jeep parked at his parents' house. So we were all
set for transporting eight people across the dunes to our
beachhead—Bobby and me, Randy and Boyfriend (who would
arrive on Saturday), Heath, John, and the two friends from

Boston.

The Friday before, John stopped by the hotel to take me shopping. He brought a *Boston Globe* with him, and it was good to feel a bit connected to the world. "You know," John said, "Queen Elizabeth is going to visit President Ford to help him celebrate the 4th. How bizarre is that? A state visit to honor one of Britain's greatest military disasters. Hmm. . . Go figure."

"Our feast will outshine the state dinner at the White House, have no fear," I assured him. I knew that John's father owned the lobster pound, so I was really looking forward to that stop on our trek. But then John mentioned that we would buy fruits and vegetables at his mother's greenmarket. "Joan, the greenmarket lady, is your mother?" I said. "Oh, shit! Anita was right. She told me the greenmarket lady had a really cute son."

"Anita is the best source of truth around," John assured me. But I was already convinced on that score.

"My mother says lobster salad needs lots of lobster—especially the meat in the knuckles—a little bit of finely diced celery, enough mayonnaise to just barely moisten it, and that's about it."

"Well, she's right, of course, but I'm going to crush the roe with the back of a spoon and mix it into the mayo. Maybe the tomalley, too. And I just feel like I have to add a little bit of thinly-sliced scallion, too. You won't tell your mom, I hope."

"Your secret is safe with me," John assured me. And indeed, I began to feel that other secrets would be safe with him, too.

Our first stop was John's father's lobster pound. "Now, behave yourself and don't embarrass me!" John said as we approached the little rise that was crowned by the rounded building with all the tanks inside.

"I'll just be my usual butch self," I assured him.

"That's what I was afraid of." John said as we walked in. The interior of the pound was lined with great tanks of bubbling seawater that kept their inhabitants cold and oxygenated, as well as sorted by size and condition. I felt that I was just about as close to the heart of the sea as is safe for a land creature, without Beebe's Bathysphere, of course.

John exchanged greetings and handshakes with two middle-aged men, and then introduced me to his father, Bill Alegria, and then to the mayor of P'town, Gene Ferreira. *Portuguese men age pretty well*, I thought, as we went through the introduction rituals. Now, there was nothing remarkable about the mayor and a local business owner having a casual meeting interrupted by the arrival of a son and the son's friend. But the sincerity of the greeting was so real that I couldn't help thinking, *This is a town that gets it. This is a town that recognizes the value of all its citizens. This is a town where gay people are an essential and cherished part of its fabric.*

John woke me from my musings—which were making me feel very silly, indeed—with some advice about lobsters. "Now, they're all good, but I suggest you stay with three pounds or under. Anything over that is too hard to cook.

They can get tough. And you want a salad, not a centerpiece. Three-pounders are actually perfect because you can get some meat out of the chambers in the body shell. Anything much smaller than that and the picking takes too long. And you can save some money buying culls—the ones with a missing claw. Today you get the family discount, too. So go for it!"

I chose two three-pound culls, and John's father threw in a third, so I knew there would be more than enough lobster to anchor our holiday feast.

Joan Alegria's produce store was always a fun place to visit. I had been stopping in, mostly on Friday afternoons, for several weeks, to see what she was able to get from her network of growers on the mainland. But knowing that she was John's mother now made the visit even nicer. *That* Friday I was shopping mostly for scallions, green leaf lettuce, the ripest possible plum tomatoes, and some very tender little cukes. But I also hoped to score a beautiful big eggplant for supper that night.

"Sorry," Joan said. "No eggplant left. I guess everyone's making that rat-tat-tooey." I settled for some just-picked pattypan squash, and we were all set.

John thanked his mother and gave her a quick kiss. And we were off. *Such a nice boy, and good to his mother*, I thought. We were quiet on our way to the little supermarket—I think it was an old A & P—in Truro. I bought a few staples, John picked out a large watermelon, and then it was back to the hotel. As we drove along, I couldn't help but reflect on how mercifully Jake-free the day had been. And I felt blessed.

John and I hauled our catch into the kitchen at the Pilgrim House, everything but the watermelon. That, he would take back to his place and inject with golden rum over the next two days, he said.

"So when do you start school?" I asked. "You said you are finishing your MS this year."

"Yes, classes start the day after Labor Day. But I need to be back before that, so I can get everything organized. There's a research project I hope to join. It's about the future of marine fisheries. It doesn't look good for fish, Atlantic or Pacific. But at least lobsters are in pretty good shape, so Dad doesn't have to worry so much."

As we stowed our purchases in the fridge and the funny old cabinets, I asked, "Do you ever get to New York?"

"Not very often, " he answered. "I like New York, but I don't really have friends there, and it can be a little intimidating."

"We could fix that," I said.

"The friends part, or the intimidation?"

"Maybe both," I replied.

John smiled and went on helping me put our groceries away. I filled the kettle and put it on a flame to heat water for coffee. John sat down and returned to the *Boston Globe* we had abandoned a few hours before. Daphne (the Kate Smith of cats), rubbed up against John's legs and purred affectionatlely.

Perhaps she was used to scoring Tender Vittles from everyone who sat at the table. No such luck this time.

"Filene's Basement has some great deals," John said. "You should probably check them out. 50% off and counting."

"It sounds like fun, but I don't really have friends in Boston, and it might be a bit intimidating," I answered.

"We could fix that," John said.

"The friends part, or the intimidation?" I asked.

"Maybe both," John said.

I made a small pot of filter coffee, and poured some into mugs. Joining John at the table, I said, "What time should we set out on Sunday?"

"I guess 10:00 will do it, don't you think?" John said.

"Sure," I answered. "We'll be ready."

Bobby walked into the kitchen, eager for a break from his charting work at the little desk in our room. "Would you like some coffee?" I asked.

"Yes, thanks," he answered. And as I was refilling the kettle, Randy walked in to gather some things from the fridge to make himself a sandwich. And then Jan and Ritchie walked in, and I added even more water and measured more coffee.

I asked Jan, "Are you sure you guys won't come with us on the picnic? It's going to be a really nice day: food, fun, Tall Ships, the whole thing."

"Oh, thanks, but we promised the boys at The Buttery we would come by for the afternoon. They ordered a suckling pig. Now, I don't mind telling you I was a bit shocked to hear talk of suckling, and pigs! But before I knew it I had accepted, and so that's that!"

"Just watch yourself, Jan," Randy said, "and don't let that pig get too close to your falsies!"

"Don't worry," Ritchie said. "I've been keeping pigs away from Jan for years."

The silliness was quite refreshing. And for at least the second time that day I said a little prayer of gratitude for Jake's absence.

Chapter Thirteen

Friends

. . . But you got to have friends.
The feeling's oh, so strong.
You got to have friends
To make that day last long. . . .

Written by Buzzy Linhart and Mark Klingman; introduced by Linhart
and popularized by Bette Midler in 1972

The morning of July 4 we were up early. Well, 9:00 AM,
which was early for us. It was a gray morning, a perfect North
Atlantic summer morning. Perhaps the cloud cover would
burn off by noon, as it so often does. There were things to
pack, and stuff to gather. My precious lobster salad was
chilling in the fridge. I had bought some rolls—from the Hot
Buns ladies—like hot-dog rolls but richer, for those who
wanted to make a lobster roll. I split them, buttered them, and
then toasted them in a big old cast iron skillet, to make them
taste just right with the lobster salad. I also packed some
sliced tomatoes, sliced cucumbers lightly vinegared, and some

green leaf lettuce.

John's mother had made fried chicken for us, which I thought was very kind, and Anita baked some lovely Portuguese almond cakes—like little cupcakes topped with chopped almonds and dusted with confectioner's sugar—and sent along some fresh berries to go with them. Bunny had offered to make his famous *crème à la crème*, but I demurred, not wanting him to go to a lot of trouble and not wanting to know what might actually be in it, in equal measure.

As Bobby and I were finishing our packing, just before 10:00, I heard the front door close behind an arriver, and looked forward to greeting John. But instead, who should walk into the kitchen but Jake, the last person I wanted to see that happy holiday morning.

"Hi, Jake," Bobby said. "What are you up to?"

"Not much," Jake answered. "Looks like you two are busy little worker bees."

"We've been invited to a picnic," Bobby said, and left it at that.

Thank you, my love, I thought.

"Then don't let me keep you," Jake said.

We won't, I thought. A very welcome front-door-slam announced John's arrival, right on time. Jake and John greeted each other with heys and hugs.

"What are you doing today, Jake?" John asked.

"Some of the other Js are having a cook-out. I'm going by there this afternoon."

"That sounds like fun. Please say hello for me."

"Will do," Jake said. And then he was off.

I breathed a sigh of relief, and remembered a lesson from my early waiter days: it's always good to have a small disaster early in the day, to get it out of the way. Then the remainder will go smoothly. I hoped this day would prove true to form.

John and Bobby and I loaded the goodies into John's Jeep, next to his watermelon that was now well chilled and generously soused with rum. John's friends pulled up in the parking lot in *their* Jeep, and then I went to get the others: Heath, who joined us in John's dune buggy, and Randy and Boyfriend, who joined the Boston contingent. The only hitch was that the guys had brought with them from Boston a beautiful big golden retriever named Rex, who immediately fell madly in love with Heath. *Of course he loves Heath. Everybody loves Heath. Man, woman, child, dog, what is it with this guy?* I wondered. The simple solution was to have the dog ride with us, so that's what we did.

We made our way out of town (on Commercial Street, of course), then headed north on a road I didn't remember that also went to the airport. That road led to a turn-off that veered to the left—to Race Point! A permit was required for off-road excursions, but John had taken care of all that. We bounced along the dunes for almost a mile until we reached a swath of beach on the north-westerly end of the Point, devoid of other people and perfectly positioned for our day's viewing of the majestic ships.

We set up camp. Actually, John brought not just a beach umbrella but a sort of tent thing. I initially remembered that Bobby christened it "Our Far Pavilion", but I double-checked it, and it turns out that the novel *The Far Pavilions* was published two years later. So Bobby must have called our tent something else delightful, and given some later beach tent the literary name. Ah, memory. Anyway, we set up the food and drink and a table for backgammon in "our far pavilion," whatever we actually called it. Our beachhead was comfy and civilized.

Once base camp was established, the coolers stashed in the shade of the tent and the beach chairs—sand chairs, they were called—unpacked, our merry band of brothers began to shed cover-ups and come out into the sunlight, such as it was, almost full flesh. Suntan lotion was applied, though I doubt that SPF existed then. I do know that Sea'n'Ski offered a bit of protection, while Coppertone was more of a frying agent. I was a Sea'n'Ski boy, of course, while Bobby and some of the others oiled up.

Bobby wore a yellow Bikini that showed off his outrageous tan, not to mention his other assets. Randy and Boyfriend wore little knit jobs like what UnderGear would call "Aussie Rower" the next decade—the "makes its own pouch" sort. Yes, it does. Heath managed to look hot in shapeless trunks. I would have preferred to see him in something skimpy, but at least I had once seen everything he was hiding that day, and was able to content myself with the memory.

John had on a kind of Hawaiian thing in bright tropical shades, which always looked great with his coloring. The Boston Boys were wearing serviceable trunks in dull colors that did not enhance their trim bodies, and did not make them stand out, either. Perhaps that was the goal? I was wearing a little red Bikini with white polka dots that were just a tad too large. I always thought that suit was a bit fey, but I knew the cut showed off my ass to its best advantage while the front dipped down just to the top of the pubes. So that silly red Bikini was always fun to wear. I could tell tales about where that suit led me over the next few years, but instead I will stick with *this* story.

It was such an easy day, devoid of pretense or pressure. It was good to see everyone so free, especially Heath running on the beach, flashing that wonderful grin with the chipped front tooth, and throwing a piece of driftwood for his new conquest to retrieve. We laughed, we ate, we drank, we splashed about in the surf. There was talk of hop-scotch, and chicken fighting, but no one was yet ready for any activities so organized.

Boston Boy I (the owner of the golden retriever) brought a volley ball and a light-weight net, a badminton net, probably. Close enough. BBI and BBII set up the net just close enough to the ocean so that the sand was compressed a bit, to give us a little traction. Randy said, "I can't believe this. I grew up just so I would never have to play ball again, and now look at me! Nolie, I guess you had better be on my team, because there's no way I can play and watch you frown across the net all afternoon." I obediently joined Randy on his side of the net, and we were opposed by Heath and Randy's boyfriend. The others decided on other pursuits, so we made up rules for a doubles game. Nothing complicated.

We served and volleyed, volleyed and served, until the points were scored and we called it a match. Of course, Heath and Boyfriend won. Randy and I didn't stand a chance. But I think I enjoyed it far more than any other game I have ever lost.

About 2:00 I went into the ocean for a swim. Not a solitary swim exactly, just a sort of mini communion with nature in all her majesty and a chance to celebrate the beauty of the day with a joyous burst of physicality. It was what I have learned to call, in those rare moments when it occurs, the sheer joy of movement. I have always been a strong swimmer. My only athletic pursuit. But that July 4th my swimming strength was of little use when I found myself moving farther and farther out to sea as I continued to swim harder and harder toward shore. Suddenly it dawned on me that I was in trouble. And with that realization came a sense of helplessness that was truly terrifying. It took our little group a moment to realize what was happening.

Heath was the one who sprang into action, because he was the one who knew what to do. Which was pretty much nothing, actually. Well, I mean *after* he quickly swam out to me and grabbed me from behind with his left arm under mine. And then the pretty-much-nothing part began. As he rolled to a side stroke, so did I. He headed us in a south-westerly direction, parallel to the shoreline. "Don't fight it!" he said. "Just let it take us where it wants to." He did not elaborate on where that might be. Across Cape Cod Bay to Plymouth perhaps? To the bottom? To the middle of the Atlantic? Heath's strong arm across my chest helped. It wasn't until later that I thought up a new line for Bunny: "Fucking is like riding a riptide: You have to relax into it if you don't want to get hurt."

But while we were in the undertow my mind was too numb for jokes. Instead we followed the current dumbly as it rounded the Point, sometimes moving out and other times moving in until, gradually, it released its grip and floated us, rather gently, to shore just around the Point from our picnic spot, beyond the light house and just before the mouth of Hatches Harbor. The others had followed our journey from the dunes. Bobby splashed out into the shallows and grabbed me. "I thought I'd lost you," he said.

"You can't lose me so easily," I told him.

John had gone to the emergency phone box to make a call. By the time the Park Patrol came barreling over the dunes, Heath and I were already ashore, drying off, sitting quietly, and having a stiff drink. I was sufficiently recovered to notice that the two Park Rangers were really hot, so I knew I must be okay. We invited them to stay for a bite and a drink, but they declined and headed back over the dunes.

Bobby had been sick with worry, of course, but it all ended so well that within an hour the ordeal was all but forgotten, by 'most everyone but me, of course. I was not only feeling exceptionally grateful—and lucky—to be alive, but also starting to develop a tiny terror in the pit of my stomach. *What if my heart just flipped for this guy, Heath, now that he is My Hero! What if I can't control my feelings and start to throw myself at My Savior? What if my life turns upside down with no better chance than landing on my head?*

I knew that for Heath it had been an automatic gesture, because he was a good and capable guy. If any other swimmer had faltered as I did, Heath would have been there with the same response. If a baby bird or a baby turtle or a maimed seagull had needed his intervention, he would have been there. If a dolphin had beached, he would have known what to do. But on 4 July 1976, I was the creature in need of support, and I was the recipient of his simple masculine competence. And, lo, these four decades later, I have never entirely recovered from the power of that EMS embrace.

In the late afternoon, after the drama had ended happily, the games had been played—wins, losses, and draws—the food eaten, the drinks drunk, the swims swum, and even a few naps napped, John checked his watch and said, "The ships are all in Boston by now, so I guess we missed the whole thing!" Well, of course we had lost the entire Tall Ships Parade to gray skies and poor visibility. But only the beautiful golden retriever with a new love cared less than I did about Tall Ships at that moment. Despite my brush with disaster, it felt like a rare perfect day. Nothing like a taste of death to make life seem all the sweeter. Even though the scheduled activity was a washout (grayout, really) we had celebrated our very own Independence Day, and it had been wonderful. I only just hoped that I still had enough of my own independence to keep my little boat on course.

Chapter Fourteen

It's in His Kiss
(The Shoop Shoop Song)

Does he love me, I want to know,
How can I tell if he loves me so?
Is it in his eyes?
Oh no! You'll be deceived.
Is it in his sighs?
Oh no! He'll make believe.
If you want to know if he loves you so
It's in his kiss,
That's where it is, oh yeah

Written by Rudy Clark, popularized by Betty Everett in 1964

"Fucking is like gambling: you have to be in it to win it."
Bunny was at it again, this time resplendent in iridescent peacock blue. Or was it iridescent peacock green? Or both? The cut of this particular costume was something right out of the '50s, a sort of I Love Lucy hostess outfit—tight bodice with fitted slacks and a long overskirt. Harlequin glasses. You

get the picture. It just begged for a cigarette holder, and Bunny had answered the cry with a long one trimmed with Rhinestones. It was campy even by his standards.

"Fucking is like reading a good book: you can always look forward to new pleasures, right up to the climax.

"Fucking is like going to school: you can always learn something new.

"Fucking is like jumping rope: timing is everything.

"Fucking is like exercise: it raises the heart rate, if you're doing it right.

"Fucking is like watching a good movie: the drama surrounds you.

"Fucking is like fishing: if you want the catch, you'd better have the right bait.

"Fucking is like sailing: time and tide wait for no man.

"Fucking is like swimming: you have to take the plunge.

"Fucking is like scuba diving: it takes a deep dive to reach the buried treasure.

"Fucking is like riding a motorcycle: the roar between your legs can be deafening." Bunny had gone beyond camp to a realm of originality that few reach.

Later that evening, after Jan's show, John stopped by to say hello to the other Js. This was a habit of his from the previous year. I marveled at how John's visits were so welcome and Jake's were so dreaded, at least by me. Just as he was about to leave, John casually asked me, "Why don't we have a coffee tomorrow afternoon? I have a book you might like to see."

"Sure," I answered. Thinking quickly, I offered, "Around 2:00?"

"Great. Meet me at the Portuguese Bakery." And he was off into the night.

The next day, I dressed with a little more care than usual for an afternoon foray onto Commercial Street. The result was just jeans and a bright turquoise T-shirt, but I knew they fit my body well and that the color brought out the green in my eyes. I can't say I was exactly titillated, but I was enjoying, very much, the thought of a flirtation while that thought was still squarely on the wholesome, innocent side of the spectrum. And then it was time to head out into the wonderful summer soup that is Provincetown.

I arrived at the bakery a few minutes before 2:00, and then John walked in perhaps a minute later. He looked rested and comfortable in his skin. I always remember that easy quality when I think of John. And his smile. It wasn't that he was deadly attractive—although he was—it was that he seemed totally at home in his life. "You have to try the fried dough," he said. "I'll order us coffee with hot milk. Is that good?" I agreed.

We went to sit at a rickety little table toward the back of the room, back from the bustle of the sales counter, and in a cool, almost dark corner. Within a few minutes the young woman at the counter brought us two steaming, milky coffees, and two big knots of puffy, bronzed dough with generous sprinklings of cinnamon sugar. It was a welcome breakfast, and indeed it was almost the beginning of the day for both of us.

As we dove into the warm donuts—*malasadas*, they are called—tearing into them and dunking them into the delicious coffee, John said, between bites, "My grandmother, the really Portuguese one, kept a food journal. She gave it to me last year, just before she died. It has all her best recipes in it. You should take a look. Her fish dishes were legendary, not just in the family, but all over town. Really."

"I believe you." I replied. "Can I see it today?"

"Sure. We can go by my place when we leave here."

I wasn't quite ready to leave the little café. "This is really good," I said.

"What is? The *malasada* or sharing it with me?" John asked.

"Oh, I meant the *malasada* with the coffee," I answered.

"In that case, I guess we'd better let you finish," John said.

We smiled at each other, and finished our breakfast in silence. Then, as we headed out into the street, I was startled by the bright sunlight that greeted us. Adjusting to the change of atmosphere as we walked to John's parents' house on the west end of town, I was feeling the contented buzz of good coffee, a fortified belly, and pleasant company to share them both.

John's parents lived in a really nice old clapboard P'town house with a bit more land than most. In back, in what had once been a stable, John had created a comfy little apartment for himself. He welcomed me into his private quarters, and I was charmed by the way he had combined some odds and ends of family furniture—an old brass bed, a small well-scrubbed kitchen table, an inviting wing chair. On the walls, he had hung old family photos, mostly sun-bronzed fishermen and work-hardened women. But there was also his parents'

wedding photo, showing a very handsome young couple looking dewy fresh in late forties fashion. I suspected that the
brass bed was their marriage bed. John didn't offer any more
information, so I let it go.

He selected a record from his collection and, taking it to the
stereo, John asked, "Are you okay with Sarah Vaughn?"

"Sure," I answered. I didn't tell him that I had heard her
once, at a small jazz club in Chicago. I decided to save that for
another time, another moment.

As Ms Vaughn became hopelessly *Snowbound*, and I marveled at the seeming incongruity of the situation, John
produced his grandmother's journal. He had already Xeroxed
her recipe for baked bluefish. "Anything else you want a copy
of, you're welcome to it," he said. "I can read her handwriting
pretty well, so just let me know if you have any trouble with
the script."

I greedily pored over Granny Alegria's book, its pages yel-
lowed with age and use. Some of the pages had slight
remnants of splatters and spills, and these were always the recipes that most caught my imagination, as I assumed they had
captured hers. There was a lot of Portuguese in the text, and I
have never learned to read it, but I was able to make sense of
many terms by comparing them to my rudimentary Spanish.

Hardly anyone, I learned later, in Spain or Portugal will
admit to any commonality in their languages (or any other traditions). But on paper at least—if not so apparent in speech—
there is an Iberian thread running through many words and
terms that even I can follow. And I had, just across the table,
a handsome reference source for the words I couldn't parse. I

quickly found another dozen recipes I would love to own, including a simple roasted cod dish that sounded perfect, and a holiday egg bread. "Just stick one of these bits of paper in the book wherever you find a recipe you like, and I'll copy it for you tomorrow," he said.

And then John kissed me. Well. Such soft lips. I kissed him back, of course. A good kiss is not such an ordinary thing that one can ignore it or pretend that it is insignificant. No, a good kiss deserves a proper response. I responded. I also laughed and tried my best to keep it a light thing. We giggled a bit, we rolled around on his old brass bed a bit, and we kissed some more. By this time Sarah Vaughn was already advising me to *Look to Your Heart*. But John tasted so nice, like coffee and cinnamon from our breakfast. And his natural scent—like sweet grass lightly bruised—mingled with the impossibly aphrodisiacal smell of summer, in an old beach house, in the arms of a very nice young man. By the time Ms Vaughn was lamenting, *I Fall in Love Too Easily*, I was beginning to wonder if I suffered from the same affliction.

Only one other time in my life, more than a decade later, was I alone with a really sweet, quality guy who kissed me with a promise of more while at least one of us was committed to another relationship, when there was no chance of its going any farther. Or was there a chance? Was I on the edge of a new life, or just trying to wreck the old one?

"I marked a dozen recipes. Is that okay?" I asked, when we had come to our senses a bit.

"Sure. I'll take it to the copy store tomorrow," John answered.

"Thanks, John. For everything," I said. Weakly. Sarah Vaughn was *Glad to Be Unhappy.* I, on the other hand, was hoping to avoid unhappiness, but not so sure I could swing it. As I headed back to the hotel, I remembered director Rouben Mamoulian's famous instructions to Greta Garbo for the final scene of *Queen Christina.* "Think of nothing," he is supposed to have advised. I decided to try that tactic. You never know.

Chapter Fifteen

Here I Go Again

Here I go again,
Heading for a heartache.
Should I count to ten,
Or close my eyes?

Lyrics by Thomas J. Wolf, Jr., music by Cy Coleman

"Truths I have had to learn the *hard way!*" Bunny was off and running, again.

"Waiters make the best fucks, and the worst partners. When you need them, they always seem to be serving someone else." Ba-dum-pum.

"He fucks best who talks least.

"Nice guys finish in a reasonable amount of time.

"Even if you are sitting on my face you can do it with grace and dignity.

"Good manners apply, especially when fucking strangers!

"It is possible for even a very elegant person to utter the words, 'Yes, fuck me! Fuck me hard!' OK, now, moving right along, we have a special birthday to celebrate tonight . . . ."

Bunny was so far over the top, I could scarcely believe my ears. But the crowd loved it, they ordered more drinks, my tips were pretty good, and so it was win/win. At the end of his act, Bunny went to the tiny dressing room to change into his street clothes—if you can call his hybrid outfits street clothes. On his way out he swept by the line where I was waiting for Anita to close out my checks. "You!" he barked, *sotto voce.* "1:00, tomorrow. And don't be late."

"Yes, ma'am," I replied, knowing that it was pointless to even consider defying an order from Bunny. Apparently, he had noticed that I was coming unglued, that I was all over the place, that I was a mess. If it was so obvious, then Bobby most have noticed it, too. Or was Bobby noticing me at all? I realized that I had lost all depth perception in matters of the heart. Bobby, Jake, John, Heath, I feared that I was losing my grip on reality. My only consolation was in hoping that if I was actually *aware* of losing my mind, then I must be, in reality, okay. Yeah, sure.

When I arrived at Bunny's the following afternoon—a few minutes early, just to be safe—my head was swimming as if I had tumbled into a great, thick soup. He sat me down and mixed up one of his dangerous concoctions. Mercifully, Bunny gave me a chance to sip the potion, to take a few deep breaths, and to settle down a bit before he began his tongue-lashing.

"Miss Saltine, you have taken leave of your senses, if indeed you ever had any. Jake is a menace, and you are ignoring him. John is a distraction, and you seem to be running to him. And Heath is a complete fantasy that you seem to think is real. So, what's next? Are you planning to become a lesbian? Because that makes more sense than the path I see you on now."

"Oh, Bunny, don't be so dramatic," I said, while at the same time absorbing his every word.

"If you think I'm being dramatic," Bunny answered, "then you don't know shit from Shinola! Honestly, Little One, why are so contrary? I can't make it work for you. No one can live your life but you. And if you fuck it up, it's your fuck-up!"

Bunny took a long breath, and then issued a quiet, measured pronouncement that is burned into my memory: "Dear Boy, and I use the term advisedly, you have the potential for greatness. You may accomplish whatever you dream. Why are you intent on squandering your resources? Why must you run hither and yon when the only truth is right here?" He punctuated his remark with a long-nailed index-finger to my heart. It was not exactly a tender gesture. In fact, it hurt. I didn't mind the pain. It was a welcome distraction from the storm that had just started in my head.

A migraine had come over me while Bunny was lecturing. I knew the telltale signs of the aura, the psychedelic squiggles of light announcing the searing pain and intense nausea that would follow in about a half hour. I made a quick exit and sprinted back to the hotel to take my pills. A few bites of cottage cheese as a stomach buffer, then three green-and-yellow capsules. *Two* might be enough for a bad headache, but there is no sense in taking chances with a full-blown migraine. I caught it just in time. Five minutes later and I would never have been able to keep the capsules down long enough for the drug to work its magic. *If only they had a drug like this for* **heart** *disease*, I lamented. No such luck.

The migraine experience forced me to lie quietly for a while. Bobby was out—sunning, of course. I had the room to myself, and so I took off my clothes and lay down on our funny old bed and thought back to Bunny's words. It was a warm afternoon, so I lay down with no top sheet at all and set an alarm for 4:30, to make sure I would be pulled together in time for work, the late shift that night. So, there was some extra, very welcome time to rest. I settled into a combination of soul-searching and napping that was calmer than anything I had been experiencing lately. The drug helped.

About 3:00, Bobby arrived from the beach, with Jake in his wake. Without any invitation I could see, Jake came in and plopped himself down on Bobby's side of the bed. I reached for the sheet but Jake was already sitting on it, so I only managed to gain enough to half cover my crotch. So much for modesty. Jake was wearing a little Bikini with pink and yellow stripes that met in the center in a chevron pattern. Jake needed no visual enhancement, but he was getting it anyway. Flip-flops. And nothing else. "Hi, Porky," he said to me. "I guess it's not beauty sleep when *you* do it." He tweaked my leg, and it was not an affectionate tweak.

"Ha, ha," was about the best I could manage. The room

had been still, but now there was something new hanging in the air like a fine mist. Coppertone and fresh sweat, mostly. A heady brew, depending on the circumstances. Now, I can normally smell sex at twenty paces, so there was nothing mysterious about what was happening. I just couldn't figure out my role in it.

Jake was obviously in no hurry to leave, and he seemed to enjoy hanging out, half sitting and half lying on the left side of our bed. Bobby's side of the bed. He watched Bobby organize his beach things, and then go to the bathroom to pee. Jake leaned in, and stretched out next to me, on his left side, supporting his very nice, very tanned head with his left hand. He was so close that I could feel his body heat top to bottom, and when he put his right leg over my legs, then it felt more like wildfire.

I willed myself not to look at Jake, but I glanced anyway. His left armpit caught my eye. The little thatch of dark hair sent a tingle through my body. Armpits had excited me since childhood when the first boys to become pubescent could show off something thrilling when they moved in their basketball jerseys. Adult armpits are even nicer: if they belong to the right man they can smell like answered prayer. Ave Maria. As my gaze lowered, it seemed to me that Jake was developing some wood in his little suit. His package was now resting on my hip bone. The fragment of sheet was no longer separating our bodies very effectively, because I was reacting to the situation, despite my appeals to my better angels.

Bobby returned, stripped off his green bikini, and walked over to me. "Are you okay, Sunshine?" he asked as he took my hand. He seemed to be ignoring Jake just as much as I was trying to.

"It was a migraine, but I caught it in time," I answered.

"Oh, good. But you need some quiet. I'll lie down, too, for a few minutes, as soon as I rinse off. Jake is just leaving, aren't you, Jake?" Bobby said.

"Sure," Jake replied.

"Okay, Jake, you take care, now," Bobby said.

"*Hasta mañana*," Jake said.

"Fuck you, too," I *wish* I had said.

"I have some work to do, so I'd better skip the beach tomorrow. Maybe the day after," Bobby said.

As Jake rose, I thought, *It is wood!* He made no effort to hide it, not that there is much that can camouflage an erection in a skimpy Bikini. In Jake's situation, his very generous penis now stood at full attention, extending well above his suit. And the perfect pink fireman's hat that crowned it seemed to be flirting with his navel. As much as I hated to take my eyes off Jake's dick, I had to glance over at Bobby to try to figure out what was happening. Bobby tried for no reaction at all, but his own penis gave him away. So, now there were *three* erections in the room, and I still had no idea what was going on.

"You can put that away now, Jake," Bobby said.

"Whatever you say." Jake smiled, while making no effort to comply. I just lay there and waited for the next move. It was Bobby's. He walked over to the door, opened it, and stood there holding the door for Jake's exit. I held my breath again. After a tense moment, Jake smirked and headed for the door. But on his way out, he grabbed Bobby by the shoulders, drew him in close, and planted a big kiss. Tongue and all, by the look of it. And then he walked out.

"That was not fun," I said after Jake was well and truly gone.

"Don't pay any attention to him," Bobby said. "He just can't resist stirring things up."

If this is stirring, I may give up cooking, I thought.

Bobby grabbed a towel and headed for the shower. I lay there and remembered an event from childhood: When I was about five, there was a little girl across the street, my age, who would be playing along nicely and then suddenly grab my arm and sink her teeth into it. This happened maybe twice. And I always felt helpless when these attacks came. Lying there on that lumpy old bed, waiting for my lover to return, and enjoying a partially-drug-induced reverie, I wondered if maybe I was still just waiting for things to happen to me, and helpless to prevent the ones I didn't want. And it also seemed clear that there must be a much better way to live.

Bobby dried off, and then lay down beside me. One part of my brain wanted to grab him, hunker down, and spend the duration of the summer with Bobby, just the two of us in our little bed. Another part of my brain was just sort of paralyzed. Paralysis got the better of both reason and desire, and Bobby and I napped side-by-side for the next hour. And then we got up and went on with our work routines.

I knew at the time, I truly knew that I had missed a golden opportunity to set things right. I knew a lot of things. And yet I couldn't seem to figure out how to do it better.

Chapter Sixteen

You're No Good

. . . I learned my lesson, it left a scar,
Now I see how you really are:
You're no good,
You're no good,
You're no good,
Baby, you're no good.

Written by Clint Ballard, Jr. First performed by Dee Dee Warwick in 1963, and covered by Betty Everett, The Swinging Blue Jeans, Linda Ronstadt, et al.

Heidi Gibson was tall and lean with a really terrific body that she seemed to be hiding. Not just a no-frills look, but a concerted effort, or so it seemed, to disappear all evidence of not just her femininity, but her sexuality. She could have been Heath's little brother. In fact they looked so much alike that it was a bit scary. And that resemblance was reinforced by their sibling-like relationship. In another age, these two would have been intended by their small-town families, married young, and locked into a passionless union. But in this age they were free to find their own way, which turned out to be brotherly love.

Heidi owned and operated a gallery just off Commercial Street on the east side of town. It was a small place, always perfectly clean and neat with whitewashed walls to make the pictures really pop. You wouldn't exactly call it dyke art that Heidi chose to display, but it was all paintings by local women artists, and they tended toward strong feminist images. Some of them were quite beautiful. Others I found a bit repellent. But I loved hanging out at Gallery Sappho because I liked Heidi, she made great coffee, and there was often the warm buttery scent in the air of the beautiful little cheese pastries she bought from the bakery next door (also dyke-owned), the source for Jan's pecan coffee cake and my lobster rolls.

It occurs to me now that maybe there was something about spending time with Heidi that somehow, weirdly, made me feel that I was closer to Heath. I know it sounds creepy, and probably a bit sick, but there is no point in denying it. I would sometimes pop in at Sappho to say hello in the afternoons if I was on my way to see Bunny or Anita. Heidi usually had time for a coffee, so I made it a point to drop in a bit early and hang out for a few minutes before heading to my destination—with a box of goodies from Hot Buns Bakery in tow.

The Wednesday after my migraine scare, in late July, I was surprised to find Heidi in an agitated state, which was just not her style. And Liz was there. Liz rarely stopped by afternoons, preferring to cycle to the beach or hang out with their large network of friends before it was time for her to go to work at The Madeira Room. And Anita was also at the gallery, which seemed odd because I was supposed to stop by her house that afternoon. I was creeped out to learn that a painting, one of the best, had gone missing from the gallery. I remembered the canvas well, a small, sensual female nude in beautiful shades of violet and green.

Heidi hadn't alerted the police. Luckily, she had the sense to call Anita, who told Moises about it. Moises knew everyone and pretty much everything, so he was a good friend to have in this, as in most all situations. Heidi was terrified of the backlash from her customers—and her artists—if news got out about a theft.

"I'm always so careful!" Heidi said. "This doesn't make any sense to me. I'm insured, of course, but that won't make it up to Sylvia if her picture disappears. And it won't make it any easier for me to get good consignments in the future."

"There has to be an explanation," Anita said.

"Don't worry, Baby. We'll get to the bottom of this," Liz assured her. We helped Heidi go over the alarm system, the door locks and windows. Everything seemed in order. Then we went over Heidi's sales book from the previous day, and started to list everyone she could remember who had been in the shop recently.

The phone rang. Heidi answered. It was quiet enough in the gallery that we could all hear that it was Moises's distinctive voice on the other end. Heidi put him on speaker-phone. "That miserable little piece of shit tried to fence it in Chatham!" Moises said. "Luckily, the gallery owners are friends of mine, and they are holding him in their back room. You know Jim and Bill at Chatham Fine Arts. They'll be glad to call the police. It's up to you, Heidi. You say."

Heidi took a deep breath. "Thanks, Moises. No, I want them to let Jake go."

Oh shit! Wouldn't you know it!, I thought.

"I just can't make any more trouble for Marie and Jen," Heidi said. "They've had enough problems this season, what with having to cancel their Memorial Day reservations because the boiler burst. No, if you haul Jake away they'll never find anyone to finish out the season. Our community is too small."

"Heidi, it's entirely up to you," Moises said.

"Let him go. But tell him to do his job and finish the season. 'Cause if he makes any trouble for Marie and Jen, I'll come for him. Tell him that."

"Sure, Heidi. I'll have the picture back to you in a few hours."

Heidi hung up the phone, took a few deep breaths, and said, "Well, that's that. You know, I'm never really suspicious of people, but I guess I should have noticed that Jake was hanging out here too long last night, that there was no reason for him to offer to help me lock up. I tried to set the alarm three times, but kept getting an error message. So, finally I called the alarm company, and they promised to send someone over in an hour. Liz, you were already at work at the club, so I went across the street to the café to have a bite while I waited. Jake left. Or so I thought.

"When the alarm girls arrived, they couldn't find anything wrong with the system, except that the back window was unlocked. So, they locked it, we set the alarm, and I went home. I didn't really go into the gallery with the alarm girls, or of course I would have seen the empty space. He's a quick little asshole, isn't he? He must have slipped something in the back window frame to kill the alarm connection while we were closing. Even a piece of paper would do it. He must have gone in that back window—any other window and I would have seen him from the café. And then he must have slipped out the window and taken the picture—and the paper—with him. Otherwise, the alarm company would have found a problem."

"The important thing is that you'll have the picture back, and it's a pretty safe bet that Jake won't cause you any more problems this season," Anita said.

"He knows he'd have to answer to both of us, and Marie and Jen, too," Liz said

"I can't thank Moises enough for this. You two have been great," Heidi said.

"Glad to help. Come on, Sunny. Heidi has had enough excitement for one day. Let's give the girls some space."

Anita and I left the gallery and headed for her house. I couldn't believe the theft was going to be swept under the rug. I was skeptical about Heidi's decision, and would have preferred to see Jake locked up far away and for a long time. But of course, Heidi didn't share my experience of Jake, and in any case, it was none of it any of my business. On the surface, at least. Heidi had made me promise not to tell anyone about it. Could I actually not tell even Bobby?

115

Ill Wind

Blow ill wind, blow away
Let me rest today
You're blowin' me no good, no good

Go ill wind, go away
Skies are oh, so gray
Around my neighborhood, and that's no good

Lyrics by Ted Koehler, music by Harold Arlen

In early August, we got word that a storm was brewing in
the Gulf, that it looked like it might very well head up the
coast, strafe even New York City, and then continue to the
Cape. Jan and the owners of neighboring businesses were
carefully monitoring the situation. They manned their TVs
and radios, and checked with fishermen and others who knew
how to tap into Coast Guard resources and such. Hour to
hour, it began to look more likely that we were actually going
to be in for a real storm. Hurricane Belle, she was called. Not
so belle, as far as I could see.

Jan and Richie asked us to help with the preparations, and so Bobby and I began to tape windows and lock down storm-shutters. It was the usual incongruity—a beautiful, sunny afternoon with no physical evidence that trouble was on the way. No doubt the birds felt it, even the seagulls. But they are on another wavelength.

Heath drove the house pick-up to Truro to get some supplies—extra fuel, bottled water, canned goods, batteries, candles, that sort of thing. Heidi went with him. I asked them to be on the lookout for a jar of pickled jalapeños and some canned tuna, just in case. We did what we could at the hotel to be useful, which was not much. The shows that night were canceled, so it was now just a waiting game.

As the afternoon wore on, we started hanging out in the kitchen, because there was nothing much else we could do. Jan, Ritchie, Bobby, me, Randy, Boyfriend (who was visiting)—we were sitting quietly, and waiting. Len was not around, because by this point he was mostly staying with a town girl he had met our first week. John stopped by to see how we were doing. "My parents and I always wait out storms at home, but this time they asked me to drive them to Providence to stay with my aunt. Just in case. We're leaving in a few minutes. Be careful, everybody. Stay indoors!" And he was off.

About 4:00 that afternoon came the phone call. Jan answered it. He went white as he listened to the caller. His half of the conversation was mostly, "Where are you now?" followed by, "How bad is it?" followed by, "Okay, I'm glad you're safe. We'll be there as soon as we can make it. God bless you, Heidi."

Jan was shaken to the core, but after taking some deep breaths he could tell us what he had just heard, which was essentially this: On the way back from Truro that afternoon a deer had darted from the scrub, forcing Heath to swerve to miss it. The pickup careened into a tree. Heidi survived the impact with little more than a small cut over her right eye, but Heath was pretty badly cracked up. The left side of his ribcage had collided with the steering column, and the damage was putting pressure on his heart. He had been unconscious ever since. The nearest hospital—then as now—was in Hyannis, and so that's where they took him. Heidi rode with him in the back of the ambulance. She phoned Jan as soon as they arrived at Emergency and got Heath admitted.

We were stunned by the news, of course. "That hospital is *built*," Jan said. "They're probably safer there anyway. And so are we. I'll see if I can find some rides for us. We should set out in about a half hour. There's no sense in hanging out here." The hotel, shuttered and airless, was becoming increasingly claustrophobic, so it did seem a really good idea to head for better shelter.

"I can take two more with us," Boyfriend said, "Three, actually." And so it was decided that Bobby and I would ride with Randy and Boyfriend, and we would stop and pick up Liz on the way. Jan walked over to The Buttery to ask the guys to drive him and Ritchie to Hyannis, which they agreed to do, in the company van. And we were off.

The drive seemed deadly long, even though it was less than two hours. But the air conditioning in Boyfriend's Buick worked great, so I tried my best to relax into the journey. There was little chitchat.

By the time we reached Hyannis, the wind had started to pick up noticeably. For the first time, it was obvious that we were in the not-so-calm before the storm. We headed into the hospital to find Heidi and get an update on Heath's condition. The Buttery Boys dropped off Jan and Ritchie, and then went to a hotel nearby.

The hospital was very quiet, with all nonessential people— staff and patients—evacuated. The ICU was on the second floor. Heidi seemed shaken, but otherwise in pretty good shape, under the circumstances. As Liz fell into her arms, I was happy that we had been able to bring Heidi some much-needed support.

The hospital staff let us go in, two at a time, to see Heath. He lay there, all pale and gingery, and so still that I had to catch my breath to keep from exclaiming. The delicate blue veins in his temples were nearly invisible now, with no sense of pulse. He looked so perfect, because the impact crushed his chest while leaving scarcely a surface scratch. A hospital gown covered the wreckage of his ribs on the left side. Doctors had done what they could to reposition bones, to reduce the pressure on his heart. The machines that were monitoring him—and sustaining him—blipped and wheezed, with sickly greenish lights that made my stomach turn.

The doctors and nurses were grave but noncommittal. And then we just had to wait. The waiting room was drab and not very comfortable. We took turns hanging out on the lumpy sofas and sitting quietly in Heath's darkened room. Bobby and I held each other from time to time. Randy and I held each other, too, with and without Boyfriend. I never did feel all that close to Jan, but while there were no embraces, we exchanged heartfelt smiles. I did get an embrace from Ritchie at one point, which seemed right, but it kind of surprised me.

Heidi was the one most devastated by the accident—because she was part of it, because Heath was her best friend, and because she had to keep his mother and his partner in Halifax updated with calls about every hour. Liz was quiet and supportive. I was glad to offer the girls a hug from time to time: woefully inadequate but better than nothing. We all felt quite helpless, as indeed we were.

Shortly before midnight Belle passed directly over us, her fury half spent by that point, but still wild enough to down local power lines. The hospital's emergency generators cut in immediately with only a minor dip and no loss of function for the machines that were keeping Heath alive. I went into Heath's room to make certain for myself that he was supported properly. The machines softly bleeped, and blinked, and ticked, and wheezed. And those icky green lights pulsed and fell. It was horrible.

Watching Heath lying there, so still, I felt a searing pain on the left side of my chest that would stick with me for at least the next week. I knew it was nothing compared to Heath's pain, and yet I felt it. *Why does it have to hurt so much?* I asked silently. But I said practically nothing aloud.

The storm raged on through the night while we waited,

with that strange window of calm in the middle, followed by more battering winds. We sat, we paced, we went to Heath's bedside, we went to the vending machines for bad coffee and peanut-butter-cheese crackers, we even tried to nap briefly on the waiting room sofas.

Eventually, Heidi said, "Let's go see the newborns." It felt good to stir from the torpor of our vigil. Heidi and Liz and I went downstairs to the nursery. It was quiet—and empty—until a nurse brought a tiny boy-child into the room and placed him carefully into a bassinet. We caught our breath.

Heidi said, "Liz, may I?"

"Of course, Heidi," she answered softly

Heidi said, "We haven't told a soul, not even Marie and Jen, but Liz just got pregnant with Heath's baby. We wanted it to be a nice surprise, in a few months, after we could be sure that things were going well. And now there's a chance that the baby might never know its beautiful father." Heidi, who had been so solid through this ordeal, began to weep softly, as did Liz. I had no more tears at the ready, but, of course, I would find them later.

Returning to the ICU, we were met with the news that Heath had died at 4:47, just as Belle was leaving Hyannis, and at the same moment the baby that Heidi and Liz and I saw in the nursery was born.

The sun rose that morning like any normal day, even more beautiful than most. The storm damage was minimal. The power was restored by 6:30 AM, and the whine of the emergency generator ceased for the first time in hours. Heidi had to make dreadful phone calls to Halifax, and arrangements for the body, of course. She was a trooper through it all, then collapsed into the backseat of The Buttery passenger van, with Liz at her side.

The drive back to Provincetown was mostly silent.

Chapter Eighteen

Early Autumn

When an early autumn walks the land
and chills the breeze
And touches with her hand
the summer trees,
Perhaps you'll understand
what memories I own.

Lyrics by Johnny Mercer, music by Ralph Burns and Woody Herman, 1949

Nothing in my past had prepared me for Heath's death. I didn't cry when my pet lizard died, or the rabbits, or hamsters, or flying squirrels. Not even dogs and cats. I did cry when I broke up with my high school girl friend, but that was because I was frightened of starting a new, rootless life. A few shames and humiliations had brought on a brief flow of hot tears down my baby cheeks. But none of this bore any resemblance to the cavernous loss that had taken up residence in my chest. When our neighbor and Cub Scout Packmaster dropped dead at age forty and we all attended his funeral in our Scout uniforms, that was close.

Bobby was also in pain, but I was not a very good partner those first days after Heath's death. *Have I ever been a good partner?*, I wondered. Sometimes when the finality of it all made me angry and I lashed out, then Bobby would naturally be the closest one to me—and the one in the way. I was angry at God even though I didn't believe in Him. I was angry at Mother Nature for sending Bambi into Heath's path. I was angry at the hospital staff for not saving him. I was angry at myself for being useless. But most of all I was angry at Heath for pitching me into this miserable hole.

Part of my reaction to Heath's death was the terrible nightmares it caused. In the worst dream, I got a call from Heidi saying she was bringing Heath home from the hospital. So, I rushed out to watch her pull up in her old pickup in front of the Pilgrim House. Heath emerged, looking a bit fragile but otherwise himself. As we helped him carefully up the stairs, the cruelty of the illusion was gradually apparent as we got Heath to his room, but it wasn't his room, exactly: it was more like a hospital room, and then the dream narrative morphed in another direction, and morphed again and again until we were driving Heath to the crematorium. I woke in a sweat, and narrowly made it to the toilet before I started heaving.

Alcohol helped, that first week especially. Interesting thing about alcohol: it doesn't exactly bring pain relief, but it can be a sort of pressure bandage that tamps down the inflammation and makes it more bearable. There was little relief from the pain for some days. And then, of course, it began to soften.

There was a service the next week, on MacMillan Pier, overlooking the bay, of course. There had been a family funeral in Halifax shortly after Heath's death. But Provincetown had had such a strong hold on him that *it* needed to memorialize him, too. Heath's mother came to P'town for the service, accompanied by Heath's partner. I heard they were coming, and I wondered how they could possibly stand it.

Bobby and I dressed in our somber best, of course. Even Bunny wore a suit to the memorial. I had no idea he owned one. We all wore suits then. Tuxedos, too. Bobby had two for work, but I had one as well, and it was trotted out two or three times a year for galas and benefits. Such a different time it was. At Heath's memorial Bunny did not, of course, disappear into his black suit. There was a hat—with veil—and a respectable amount of jewelry. As Betsy Palmer once said, "Face it, darling. You can't hide the glow!"

Anita and Moises joined us. It occurred to me that this was harder for Anita than it was for me, and the realization forced me to be a bit stronger. The entire Pilgrim House family showed up, of course, as did at least half the town. I caught sight of Heidi and Liz encircled by a bunch of friends, and I felt glad they had support. John and I waved to each other from a distance. We had made a plan to get together later for a drink.

Meeting Heath's mother—who was also tall, handsome, and gingery—was difficult for me. I managed something lame

127

like, "We all loved your son," and then I moved along the receiving line to Heath's partner. He was not exactly what I had pictured. Instead of a rugged type, I was introduced to a gentle man, about my height, with a slight but strong build. He was fair, almost blond, with soft blue eyes that were wells of grief at that moment. I liked him instantly, as my heart rushed out in a vain attempt to buoy his. In a matter of seconds, I processed a jumble of feelings, including sorrow for his loss, sorrow for *my* loss, regret that I would probably never get the chance to love this beautiful man, and guilt that I had ever even in the remotest corner of my brain wished to take his place.

"Heath touched so many lives," was about the best I could manage. And then I moved on. And, so did my conscious brain. For in that moment, I really knew that it was over and Heath was gone. I looked over at Bunny and Anita and thought, *This is too much like our last trip to MacMillan Pier.* I wondered how Anita could bear this repetition of life and death events all marked in almost the same way. And yet even as I marveled at her strength, I began to feel lifted by the ritual, the sense of community, the orderly process of beginnings and endings. Ceremonies, indeed. Well, how the hell else can we get on with it?

No one could have known that Heath's memorial was only a precursor of all the memorials to come. As I look back on it now, writing about it is more difficult and more painful, more of an open wound than the scores of memorials I later attended, starting in the early '80s, when dead gay boys became the new normal. A decade-and-a-half of early deaths never made it feel any easier, but it certainly lost the element of surprise. Lest I sound flippant, let me assure you I am acutely aware of the suffering of the victims, their survivors, and their caregivers. But forgive me, I'm getting ahead of myself.

Acceptance? No, not really. No, I have never accepted Heath's death. Never found resolution in the naturalness of the cycle of life. Never wanted to think about God's will. Never learned to accept the rightness of all that happens in the universe. Never could, hard as I've tried. But that summer, as I mourned the loss of Heath, I had an issue even more pressing than grief. I was living in a state of uncertainty about my relationship, and my entire future. And I still didn't quite get it.

Chapter Nineteen

Don't Pull Your Love Out on Me Baby

Don't pull your love out on me baby
If you do then I think that maybe
I'll just lay me down and cry for a hundred years. . . .

Written by Brian Potter and Dennis Lambert, introduced by Dan Hamilton, Joe Frank Carollo, & Tommy Reynolds in 1971

The week after Heath's memorial, Heidi had a gallery opening. The event had been scheduled the month before, so even though Heidi was still devastated by Heath's death, she knew that he would want things to go on as normally as possible. She decided to dedicate the show to Heath's memory, and one of her friends, fortunately, had painted a portrait of him the year before. And while it was not for sale, the beautiful little canvas would make a touching centerpiece for a tiny "altar" that Heidi set up in the middle of the gallery.

There was also another canvas, larger, also not for sale, and not for public view, either. But Heidi showed it to me, the day before the event. This painting, by the same artist who did the little portrait, was a nude that Heidi had asked her to paint. It was meant to be a Christmas gift for Heath's boyfriend, but when Heidi saw it finished, she couldn't bear to part with it. And so they had planned to arrange another sitting *this* summer, to produce a belated gift. It had even been started. And then everything changed.

Seeing the pretty little portrait was hard enough, but when Heidi showed me the nude, I was what is now called gobsmacked. Fresh anger, fresh grief, fresh consternation. The canvas was so beautiful, and so Heath-like. I thanked Heidi for sharing it with me, tried to behave like a wise and generous friend, and failed miserably at providing anything like support. The best I could do was put my sunglasses back on and head out. But before I left I promised to bring her some nibbles for the party.

The afternoon of the opening, I headed down to the Madeira Room to set up my station early, to get it out of the way so that I could go out for the afternoon and enjoy the opening. I had also prepared some little toasts topped with lemon-juice-cured raw salmon slices, a little minced shallot, and a caper. Paintings, wine, food, interesting people—it seemed time to get on with it.

I straightened my tables. There was a creak on the back stairs, and as I turned with a startled jerk, there was Jake. "Jesus, Jake. Where did you come from?"

"From your ex-boyfriend's bed, of course. Just ask him when he comes down here to work at the piano."

Jake was wearing a little tank-top and some short shorts, with nothing underneath, by the look of it. If someone had said, "Study this picture. What do you see?" I would have said, "I see a hot guy who just finished having fabulous sex, wiped his cock off on the bedspread, and then slipped back into his shorts—but only because he might get arrested if he went out on the street without them." In fact, Jake always looked as if he would be much happier naked, as I am sure he would be, as I am sure many around him would be, too. Unfortunately, I must count myself in that camp, though I would prefer not to have to admit it.

Jake advanced on me slowly, obviously relishing his advantage. Now, I won't say that I was getting an erection, but I won't say that I wasn't, either. The air was so still in the half-light of the empty club that Jake's scent only reached my nostrils when he was already dangerously close. His now familiar sex-on-the-beach aroma only increased the dizziness I already felt.

"Give it up, Chub," he said in a hoarse whisper. Even his breath was pheromonic.

"Leave me alone, Jake," I managed.

"No, *you* leave *Bobby* alone. It's over, you know." And then he grabbed my crotch. It was a menacing gesture, and a little painful. I winced. He laughed when he realized that he had grabbed something firm rather than pliant. And then Jake bit my neck, while still gripping my dick. That hurt, too. I can't for the life of me tell you how he did it, but the next thing I knew, Jake had slipped handcuffs onto my wrists, so that my arms were pinioned behind me. Now, I had seen a

133

little kink before, but I had never been in an actual handcuff, and I have no idea how he managed it. Pulled them out of his back pocket, I suppose. And like greased lightning he bit, and squeezed, and locked my wrists.

Once Jake had overcome me physically (as well as emotionally), it was a simple matter for him to spin me around and push my chest down onto one of my tables. He chuckled as he slipped my pants down toward my ankles. And then there was no longer any question where this scene was headed.

I was as terrified as I have ever been, of course. But there was a voice within, from some deep survival region, that said to me, "**If you want to come out of this intact, you must accept it.**" And that is exactly what I did. I relaxed everything I had. I relaxed parts I didn't even *know* I had. I went into deep-breathing mode that was positively Zen.

Next, I felt something hot, wet, and probing. Jake was rimming me! I accepted it. And I prayed that the lubrication would save me. Jake's first thrust *might* have sent a thrill of pain all the way up to my teeth. But instead, I accepted it. I would not be victimized. I would not be bloodied. I accepted the violation. I even smiled. Not so much as a whimper from me. When Jake pumped harder, I found more stillness in my core. When he went into long, slow strokes, I visualized my acceptance of each penetration and each withdrawal.

When he leaned forward onto my back, pushing my arms into a painful configuration, I relaxed my shoulder joints in new ways. And when he lay on top of me and pressed his face to mine and filled my lungs with his hot breath, then I accepted that, too. And when he grew frenzied and irregular with his strokes, and hissed, "Yes, take it, Pig," then I took it.

The thrusts that followed were intense, but no longer angry. And when Jake arched his pelvis to achieve maximum penetration, I accepted him fully. I even held my breath so that I could present him with perfect stillness. Jake seemed to freeze in place, the only motion now the throbbing that emptied him and filled me. I welcomed each pulse. I became a perfect vessel.

When Jake relaxed his torso down onto my back and put his arms around my head and shoulders, I accepted his embrace. He lay there, in me and on me, for God knows how many minutes. I accepted that, too. My humiliation was complete. And then it was over.

I knew, of course, that Jake came inside me. One can tell, I think. I know I can. I didn't mind it. I was proud of my strength. And what Jake had planted seemed to belong there just as surely as if we had made love. Instead of being diminished by it, I felt empowered. Even though it came from violence, it came from deep inside Jake's body. It was the best he had to offer, and I accepted it. And I earned it. And I wanted to hold it inside me for as long as I could.

How long did the assault last? Five minutes? Thirty minutes? I have no idea. But as quickly as he had started, Jake released my wrists, took a step backward, buttoned his shorts, and started to laugh. "I'll never know what Bobby saw in you," he said. "But he's with me now, so get used to it."

I pulled up my pants, then rubbed my wrists to try to encourage the circulation. But my blood supply, which had been favoring my crotch, began to reroute itself and engorge my brain instead, where it was truly needed. It was a long time coming, but I finally found my voice.

"Jake," I said. "You have caused enough trouble around here. Everybody is on to you. *Everybody*, including Bobby. I want you out of my face, and out of my life, or. . ."

"Or what? What are going to do, Fat Boy?"

"I'll see you in jail before I spend another day letting you intimidate me!"

Just at that moment Bobby called out from the half-darkness at the top of the stairs: "He's right, Jake. You need to leave here, now. And you need to stay away from us. Permanently."

It wasn't that simple, of course. Jake did not play nice. As Bobby came down the stairs, Jake walked over to meet him. Jake said quietly, "Let's go now, Baby." He had placed himself exactly between me and Bobby. "You don't need that mess anymore," he said gently, a slight toss of his head indicating the mess who was standing behind him. He tried to caress Bobby, quite tenderly, actually. It was horrible.

"Jake, you're not listening," Bobby said. "Out! Now!"

"But Baby, it's going to be so good," Jake promised.

"Out!" Bobby repeated.

"But Bobby, we belong together!" Jake insisted.

"Jake, are you out of your fucking mind? If you want to leave this room alive, you'll do it now."

It seemed that Bobby had landed his point. Jake sputtered a bit, along the "It's your loss," line, and then he was gone.

Bobby walked over and put his arm around me. I was feeling shaky, now that the crisis had passed, and Bobby seemed rattled as well. He hugged me and I hugged him back. We maintained our embrace for a minute while we both tried to normalize our breathing and to regain our equilibrium. How much had Bobby seen? None of the rape, surely. Or he would have stopped it. Just the confrontation after.

"It's over, Sunshine," Bobby said.

"What's over?" I asked.

"The whole Jake thing," Bobby answered.

"You're sure?" I asked.

"Certain," he assured me.

So what was the whole Jake thing, from Bobby's perspective? I have no idea. I didn't ask. I didn't need to know anything more than the few hazy facts on the table. Bobby said it was over and that was that. And after all, I was hardly in a position to take the moral high ground.

I finished setting up my station, then headed for the shower. As I lathered up, a wave of sadness flowed over me, almost as palpable as the warm water. I realized that I was feeling sorrow because Jake's achingly beautiful penis *should* have been a source of pleasure, joy, even celebration, for him and for others. But instead he used it as a weapon. His member was worthy of respect—even adoration—but he was not. And there it was. I mourned the wasted resource, and then I gently released Jake's gift. As it flowed away, the emotional residue of the day flowed with it. And then it was almost as if the

137

whole thing had never happened. I dried off and dressed, and then Bobby and I headed out to Gallery Sappho with my salmon canapés in hand.

When Bobby and I arrived at the gallery, Heidi seemed positively radiant. I had never seen her so animated. More than two dozen people were milling about, inside and outside the gallery, drinking wine, munching on various snacks (what James Beard used to call "dits 'n' doots"), talking, looking at paintings, and—here is the best part of all—buying pictures! Three of the best had already been spoken for, and Heidi seemed confident that at least two more of her customers might actually pull the trigger before the party's end.

The little station that Heidi had set up in the middle of the gallery with the portrait of Heath in the center was perfect. It had just the right sense of respect and honor without falling over the edge. It occurred to me that it was just as strong and modest as Heath himself, and I caught my breath whenever I glimpsed it out of the corner of my eye.

Heidi thanked me for the canapés. Liz arranged them on a plate and started to pass them around. The response was enthusiastic—"You're a fucking genius!" Liz said—and I must confess that I was hungry for the feedback. I often wonder if I lack the depth to give a significant gift. Is my heart too shallow? What if all I have to offer is something that I craft with my own two hands. Does that count? I'm now getting into Little Drummer Boy territory. Pa-rrrum-pa-pum-pum. But maybe those of us who cook always wonder about how we relate to others. How we share with our friends is a big fucking deal, and I was feeling just a bit soft around the edges on account of having recently been forced to reexamine the gifting process.

We hung out as long as we could and met a few artists and visitors, too. Including a very cute couple from Chicago who used to eat in a restaurant where I had worked. Nearly everyone we knew in Provincetown stopped by Sappho Gallery in the next hour. And then Liz walked back to Pilgrim House with Bobby and me, and we three went to work.

❦

That night, after work, Bobby and I met back in our little room with a view, undressed, and prepared for bed. As I came down from the buzz of the day's events, I felt a little shudder as I relived an instant from the assault. And then I thought, *Bobby was right. The whole Jake thing is over.* And at that moment I knew I would be okay.

I also hoped that *we* would be okay. It occurred to me that I had always been an all-in kind of guy, whether it was an orgy or a tea party. Once committed, I was 100%. I thought that was the relationship I had found with Bobby. I never understood long-distance, part-time, or casual. My heart doesn't work that way. It wants it all. But there I was in a strange setting where I didn't quite know what was going on, and the only one I could *really* talk to about it was Bobby. And he was the one I was afraid to broach the subject with.

139

Bobby and I didn't really talk much that night, but we were able to regain some of our sense of you-and-me-against-the-world, which I think all couples require if they are to survive. It made the events of the following days easier to navigate.

Chapter Twenty

Goodbye John

. . .Farewell my fair, my own, my bonny,
Farewell my handsome, winsome Johnny.
If I cry, it won't show.
Goodbye, John, don't go!

Lyrics by Edward Eager, music by Alec Wilder, introduced by Peggy Lee in 1949

This is so silly, I thought. John leaves for Boston today, and we head back to New York in two weeks, and everything is exactly as it should be. But no matter how I reminded myself of the rightness of the situation, the little achy thing above my diaphragm reminded me that life is not always so neat.

John asked me to go with him to the airport, then drive his Jeep back to his parents' house. I agreed, of course. I would have preferred to say goodbye to him the day before, at the hotel, perhaps. With other people around. I had learned in theater school that the real drama in life is in arrivals and de-partures—beginnings and endings. The rest is mostly, "What's for dinner?" I would gladly have missed *this* ending in ex-

141

change for a bit less drama around the heart.

Instead, it was going to be a real departure. Not exactly *Now Voyager*: no wilted camellias, no train steaming and whistling and slowly chugging out of the station. Nothing so Hollywood as that. It was just an everyday departure.

"Why don't you come to see me?" John said as we approached the airport road. "You'd like Boston."

"I'm sure I would," I said. Things I did *not* say: "Any city with you in it would be a great city," or "As long as we can spend some time together, just the two of us," or "Please don't forget me."

"It's not New York, but I really like living there," John said.

"Maybe next summer," was my lame reply. And then we were silent.

We pulled up in front of the airport ("The White Zone is for the immediate loading and unloading of passengers only"), we got out, and John took his bags from the back of the car. I gave him one hug and a quick kiss, and he headed into the little terminal as I got behind the wheel of his Jeep. He turned back once and waved before he disappeared. I was grateful for the wave. Anything more and I might have gotten really stupid.

Driving back toward town, I began to sob. It was just a slight hiccupy thing to start. Nothing to worry about, I hoped. But then it took hold of me, and I had to slow down to the point that a driver behind me was honking. I pulled over, off the airport road onto the soft shoulder, secure in the knowledge that John's all-terrain tires would get me out of even the worst sand trap. I sat for several minutes, hoping that behind my sunglasses I might appear to anyone driving by to be some tourist enjoying the scenery rather than a weeping idiot. A plane started its ascent from the runway at the funny little airport. It was most likely John's flight. It wasn't as if there were many.

As the clatter of the propellers gradually softened to a gentle buzz, and the body of the plane shrank into the western horizon, I began to feel nearly human again. John would be in Boston in a few minutes. Home. I would be back at the hotel in a few minutes, back to my precious mate, back for an early dinner, and then to work on time. And that was that.

Looking back on that moment and trying to write about it proved more difficult than I expected. While I don't believe in regrets and rarely second-guess my choices, John is a rare "what if?" in my life. What if I had allowed myself to fall in love with a very nice, very attractive young man my own age in Provincetown in the summer of '76? What if I had thrown my bonnet over the mill and escaped my happy life for a new one with no promise of happiness beyond a fresh young dream? What if?

The nostalgia I feel is not just about John and me, but rather about all the beautiful young men that season, those of us who were privileged to grow up and grow old, as well as those who were cut down in their prime. I don't know if anyone who was not there can really appreciate the sweetness of those times and those boys. But even so, I am compelled to write my story and to try to communicate it the best I can.

Of course young people today have that freshness, too. But those boys, in the summer of '76, were so gloriously *young,* and I among them, with a wonderful innocence about us, even as we were doing our best to fuck each other silly. I always thought we were part of a continuum out of the 1960s that led to the Summers of Love and to the end of the war, etc. It felt so free! The party was long and lush, and the hangovers were mostly mild. Perhaps it was too good to last. Perhaps even if the epidemic had not struck, there would have been another, less horrific way to end the era. But end it would.

Chapter Twenty-One

With so Little to Be Sure Of

It was marvelous to know you
And it isn't really through.
Crazy business this, this life we live in.
Can't complain about the time we're given.
With so little to be sure of in this world,
We had a moment.

Written by Steven Sondheim for *Anyone Can Whistle*, 1964

That last Sunday morning, I got up a little earlier than usual and headed to the kitchen to make coffee for Bobby and me. Randy was already in the kitchen, preparing some breakfast for himself and Boyfriend. It felt good to be alone with Randy, and I realized that our whole summer together had been mostly work and group activities. A moment for just the two of us felt really nice.

"It was quite a summer, Randy," I said.

"Well, I must say, you brought some spice to it, Miss Magnolia," Randy said. "You know, I have to tell you, I think you are perfect for Bobby. I love seeing you two together. I predict a long and loving future!"

"Oh, Randy, you have no idea how good it is to hear that. I don't always know if I can trust my instincts," I said.

"Well, you can trust your heart. And your dick, of course. Let's not leave him out of this."

"Of course," I echoed. "I'm really going to miss you guys."

"Now don't go all weepy on me. We live in the West '90s, so we're mostly just across the Park from each other. We can get together whenever you like."

I wondered if Randy really believed that we would become new best friends, after our return to real life. I wondered if *I* believed it. Summer flings are notoriously impermanent. I hugged Randy, hard, and when we parted it seemed to me that he was getting a little weepy, too.

"Smile, Magnolia!" he chided me one last time. And then our farewell was interrupted by mates and house-mates, and it would soon be time to go our separate ways.

Jan showed up in the kitchen while we were breakfasting. It was, after all, his kitchen. Seeing him puttering about at the stove, it occurred to me that I had been wrong to mistrust Jan, that even without walking a mile in his pumps, I should have accepted him at face value. The kindly old queer that he presented was more or less his reality. And there was no reason for me to doubt it. He delivered on all his promises: there was a room, there was work—with set hours—and Bobby got paid on schedule. We waiters were scarcely paid at all, but that was standard in those days, and the tips were the main focus. I was used to that. So as gigs go, this one was nearly perfect.

"I can't believe there are only two more performances," Ritchie said as he walked in. "Full houses for both. Maybe we can squeeze in a few more people. Do you think they would mind swinging from the rafters?" I looked around the kitchen, taking it all in, seeing Randy, Boyfriend, Ritchie, Jan, Bobby, and Daphne, of course. I said a simple goodbye to all of it (except for Bobby), and then I just let go. The Pilgrim House was no longer mine, and so I returned it to Jan.

The week before, Bobby and I had been window shopping on Commercial Street when we decided to enter a nice little jewelry store. One of a Kind, I think it was called. Old, collectible, used, estate jewelry. The owner, Doris, greeted us warmly, and we started looking around. We quickly found a sterling baby rattle that would make a great gift for Heidi and Liz. Doris cleaned it up a bit and put it in a little velvet pouch, so we were pleased that we now had our baby gift. And we also bought puffy little gold hearts to add to our neck-chains: in this case Doris happened to have *two* of a kind. And we joined Doris's mailing list, too. She kept up with us for years to come.

There was another couple in the store that afternoon. The elder of the two was fairly tall and rail-thin, with almost-white hair and a trim beard. His most striking feature was a very large nose, and it seemed to be echoed in the equipment below, judging by the bulge in his jeans. The younger guy had a softer look, with light brown hair and smooth features. He was tall, and moved like a dancer. The older guy was choosing an emerald stud and preparing to have his left ear pierced. Doris expertly popped in the little trainer stud, and he was all set. Then he said to his partner, "OK, Beetle. You're next."

"Are you kidding? No way," replied the dancer.

"But you said you wanted to get a piercing with me."

"No, I said that if you wanted to do it, then I'd go with you." And then they both started to laugh. And it seemed to me that they were very much in love.

Now, I can't tell you right now why I chose to share that little story, but I do hope, Dear Reader, that you will file it away in your memory banks and trust that eventually, all will be revealed.

That last Sunday afternoon, Bobby and I stopped by Sappho to see Heidi and Liz. We had put the silver baby rattle in a little box, and we had found a card, too. The girls greeted us warmly and oooed and ahhhed over the gift. I think they really liked it for itself as well as the gesture. And I was relieved by the thought that we had chosen well.

"I can't believe we're leaving in a few days," I said. "I'll miss this place, and your coffee, Heidi. And I don't know what I'll do without those little cheese things."

"I'll ask the girls if they would consider parting with the recipe. As long as you give them credit. And don't try to set up next door," Heidi said.

I assured her I was good with all of the above, and then we

started our goodbyes. Bobby and Liz had two more shows together, but this was likely our last meeting with Heidi. Leaving that relationship behind was even harder for me than I had anticipated.

As I looked around at the tidy little gallery, it occurred to me that Heidi and Liz were doing a remarkable job of keeping things together and remaining upbeat, for the sake of the pregnancy, of course, but also because they were obviously survivors with a whole future to consider. The little portrait of Heath had been moved to a permanent place of honor (and clearly labeled Not for Sale). And I knew that they would be okay, and that Heath's child would bless their lives for years to come. I wondered if I would ever see them again. I accepted that I might not. And then Bobby and I headed back to the hotel.

As we walked, Bobby said, "You know, Liz is not a great drummer. But whenever I start to get peeved at her, I remember how much I love their relationship. I've seen some dyke violence through the years, believe me. Gay men, rarely; women, often. But those two are so loving that it just makes me want to give Liz a pass. And she has a great laugh."

Well, I wasn't so sure about the ratio of violence between gay men or between gay women, but I was more than willing to celebrate Heidi and Liz's union.

᪦

"You know, I haven't been to New York in twenty years. Moises and I took Paul there one winter. We wanted him to see the museums, especially. It was hard enough to get him out of the Fine Arts when we were in Boston, but in New York, at the Metropolitan, he was ready to camp out. It was a good trip. It would be hard to do that again, without Paul. But maybe." I had asked Anita to come and visit. It seemed unlikely, but I was having a really hard time cutting the cord. I felt so invested in her life that I couldn't quite imagine leaving that relationship behind. Now, I had a mother of my own, and every reason to expect that we two would have a long future together. But Anita was here and now, with no guarantee of any future whatsoever. And I was not dealing very well with the realities.

We were having a glass of Madeira. Rainwater, this time. Light, very nice. Moises joined us at the big old pine table in the middle of that warm kitchen.

"What a summer," I said.

"You and Bobby will be off to something quite different next summer, I expect," Anita said. "But, Sunny, just in case you two want to join Jan's season again, we would love to see you."

"Thank you," was about the best I could manage. "I'd love it, too."

As I rose to leave, Anita embraced me warmly, and kissed me full on the mouth. And then she left the kitchen by the back door and headed out into her garden. Moises saw me to the front door. I turned to extend my hand, but in place of a handshake, Moises locked me into a surprise bear-hug. "God-speed," he said. And then I was off, back to the hotel.

On Monday afternoon, Bunny and I met for a goodbye drink. Not at his place this time, but at a little neighborhood bar. Bunny ordered a beer, and when I expressed surprise he said, "Man cannot live by Pink Ladies alone." I joined him. I like beer, but I never think to order it. Most likely we drank Bass Ale, or something else with a nice hopsy base note. It was cold, and very refreshing.

"You grew a little this summer, Little One," Bunny said.

"What do you mean?" I asked.

"I want to see you become the best faggot you can be. You're not there yet, but you made some progress. Major progress, actually. I guess I'll have to call you Old Man, now." We sipped our beers in silence. And then it was time to leave.

On the sidewalk in front of the bar, I reached out and embraced Bunny, for the first time, actually. His response was guarded, but he did allow the squeeze.

"Thanks for everything, Bunny," I said. I mean, what else is there to say, really?

"If there is ever anything I can do to help, just ask," Bunny said quietly. And then he turned his back and walked away. And he did not *sashay* away, either. He just walked. Elegantly, of course. And as I saw Bunny disappear around a slight bend in Commercial Street, I felt a coldness grip my bowels even though the sun was still shining just as warmly as before our leave-taking. I sensed that I might never see Bunny again after tonight's show, and that I might never again have a friend of his caliber. And my premonition was accurate on both scores.

Chapter Twenty-Two

Carry Me Back to Old Manhattan

Carry me back to old Manhattan,
That's where my heart belongs.
Give me a show spot to hang my hat in,
Sing me those Broadway songs.

Carry me back to old Manhattan,
Far from that harvest moon.
I can't adjust to the rustic pattern,
I'm not myself till noon.

I prefer glamor dressed in satin,
Keep your calico.
So, carry me back to old Manhattan
And never let me go!

Lyrics by Douglas Cross and Peter Windsor, music by George Cory

"I want to talk about slings." One last show for Bunny, and he was going to wrap things up in high style. "Now, for the tourists in the house, this is nothing to do with a broken arm. No, this is a rectangular—more or less—piece of black leather with reinforced holes in the corners so that you can hang it from the ceiling. With *chains*. *Thick chains*! Now this contraption hangs about this high," indicating crotch height, "and it is always suspended in a place of honor. It might even have a spotlight. Because there is considerable drama taking place on and around this sling, and no one should miss out because it is too dark. For a sling to work properly, you need a minimum of two men. But there is plenty of room around the sling for, let me see, one, two, at least three more participants, and then a half dozen or so voyeurs. So, we can consider this a group effort.

"Now, the first man, who is called the bottom—or the slingee—sits down on one side of the sling—this is now the front of the sling—and then lies back on the leather. He raises his legs and places them on the two front chains, one on either side. Hell, there might even be stirrups provided for his convenience. Now, the slingee may grasp the remaining two chains with his arms, as needed, but there really should be other things for him to do with his hands, as we shall see. After all, idle hands . . .

So when the slingee is in place, the slinger approaches the front of the sling and, after an optional bit of foreplay, begins to do things to the slingee, using various body parts. Other participants may gather around the sling, offering encouragement, tit play, poppers (next lecture), and additional dicks for the slingee to handle (this is where we keep those hands busy) and whatever else he might do with them. The performance continues until the slinger has had enough, steps away, and is replaced, perhaps by one of the participants who has patiently waited his turn while performing a subordinate role on the side. This process may continue for quite a long while, until there are no more slingers in the queue or the slingee elects to stand up—with some help from others, usually—and leave the stage.

"So, what is a sling, Boys and Girls? It's a Lazy Boy Recliner!" Ba-dum-pum. Was Bunny trying out new material? Had he saved this one up for the last show? I knew better than to second-guess anything he did.

Just as Bunny came off stage, I happened to catch something out of the corner of my eye. Well, sure enough, Jake had stopped by for the last performances. And yet, I had not felt—or smelled—his presence. He was just there. And it didn't much matter one way or another. The house was packed, and I was much too busy to dwell on my reaction to Jake's arrival. And yet I sensed that I had had no reaction at all, and that that was a good thing.

Tuesday morning was quiet. We saw Randy and Boyfriend off, and then retreated to the kitchen, where we sipped coffee and finished reading the Sunday New York Times. We had accepted a ride home from an old friend of Bobby's, who would be leaving Provincetown the next morning—in a large car, luckily. And so we had the whole day to ourselves to pack at a leisurely pace and then do whatever we wanted to do. I always used to work up considerable nerves on travel days. But I had just about figured out that loading out of a hotel is a whole lot less stressful than packing for a trip. Leaving requires no decisions: throw *everything* into a bag and you are done.

That evening, we made one last appearance at the bar at Plain & Fancy, for one last vodka Gibson on-the-rocks. And then we went to a diner that specialized in lobster rolls. I just felt that I needed one more lobster roll to hold me until the next time, whenever it might be. Bobby indulged me, giving up his "proper dinner" for snack food that evening. It was delicious. We had a really good time, and laughed easily and often.

When we got back to Pilgrim House, Bobby asked me to sit (on our only chair), poured a Scotch for me and a vodka for himself, and walked over to sit on the edge of the bed. "Sunshine, I want to know where we're headed. I want to know if you're sure that I'm what you want, that it's enough."

Bobby was entirely non-confrontational, and there was a sadness in his eyes that clutched at my throat. The surprise of it caught me off-balance, and my first reaction was to feel almost as though I had been caught in a lie and needed to invent another to cover it. Except there were no lies. Bobby was a smart man, and a highly intuitive one. And he wanted it to be right.

I began to sputter a bit, and started in with some the-lady-doth-protest-too-much reactions. Bobby waited patiently until I settled down. And then what happened that evening was that Bobby forced me to go deep and find the truth at the bottom. And that truth was that Bobby was it.

I thought of my grandmother after we buried my grandfather, when she came out from the kitchen in her Hollywood, FL, co-op—where she had been preparing ice cream sodas, like the old days—to announce, "Don't think I'm going to take up with someone else, like so many women around here. I had my man!" I never had Grandma's style, never had the tear just about to fall from the left eye at the crucial moment. But I was certainly heading in that direction the evening that Bobby sat down on our funny old bed in the Pilgrim House Hotel in Provincetown, Massachusetts, just after Labor Day, 1976, and gently demanded to know my intentions. I freely affirmed that I still wanted what we had started in Chicago the November before, that I wanted to spend the rest of our lives together. And I meant it—every syllable, every word, every heartbeat.

The End

In My Life

There are places I remember
All my life, though some have changed,
Some forever, not for better,
Some have gone and some remain.
All these places have their moments
With lovers and friends I still can recall.
Some are dead and some are living.
In my life, I've loved them all.

Written by John Lennon and Paul McCartney for the album _Rubber Soul_, 1965

It wasn't until years later, when everything had changed, that I realized how much sex there was in the '70s. I had friends who couldn't make it to the supermarket and back with a few groceries without an encounter. It might be a quickie in a public john or actually going home with some neighborhood guy for a more purposeful exchange of bodily fluids. Whether fast or slow, it was inevitably frequent and light-hearted. I loved it. It felt so simple and natural. There were lasting relationships that came from those encounters, too. Nearly every couple, even the twenty-years-plus kind, had met at a bar or the baths. It was fuck first and ask questions later. And it felt so right.

And yet, through it all, we also managed to forge careers, friendships, families, homes, devotion to the arts, and other human and humane pursuits. We built solid and enduring lives where no blueprint existed. We were not so politically active, though. That would wait for the necessities of the next decade and beyond.

Even though the Summer of '76 was so long ago and so generally insignificant in the grand scheme of things, it colored my future and lives within my heart to this day. It was a child-hood of sorts that I had been living, but then never could quite sustain afterward. The events of that summer chipped away at the armor of invincibility that protects all children, or rather all children who have reasonably ordinary childhoods.

It seems to me that children who grow up with violence, abuse, and deprivation develop other, thicker armor, which protects them and allows them to grow and prosper, provided it is a good fit. But the boringly normal children—even the gay ones—are buoyed and encased by the unquestioned belief that they will live forever. And they wear this armor lightly, carelessly, trivially, right up until the moment when experience snatches it from their bodies, dashes it upon the rocks of reali-ty, and leaves them naked. As if they were molting blue crabs shedding their shells, they are particularly vulnerable—and sweet—until they have managed to grow a new one.

The new shell is roomier, allowing for growth. It doesn't

fit at first. We must grow into it. It is not so different, really, from the old shell. A bit stronger, yes. The basic functions and colors are the same. We don't really look different, at first glance at least. But the heart has undergone a sea change. And we will never be the same.

I have heard several stories through the years about men of my parents' generation, relatives and friends, who were never the same after WWII. These were joyous, funny, free-spirited boys who went off to war and returned as sober, somber young men. The horrors of war are highly effective agents of change. But life can do that, too. Just Life, as she is lived. The summer of '76 was that for me, and for others as well. It was good preparation for the myriad losses of the next two decades, if indeed there is any effective preparation for watching the best and brightest culled by an epidemic. But that—as they say—is another story.

This is a first edition from
Audacity Books
Please visit us on the web at
www.audacitybooks.com
For information, please send your request to
info@audacitybooks.com.

YOU'RE SURE TO FALL IN LOVE is the first volume in
Bruce K Beck's **Love Trilogy**, to be followed by *LOVE AND
THE EPIDEMIC*, set in New York City in the mid-'80s, and
the finale, *AND LOVE ENDURES*, set in the early 1990s. For
updates, please subscribe at **www.audacitybooks.com**.

Many thanks to Sonya Teclai, Social Media Director at Audacity Books, for her support throughout the project. Particular thanks to Kathie DeNobriga and Lukas Hassel for their generous wisdom. And to Richard Kutner for his classy edits. Tim Barber of Dissect Designs (www.dissectdesigns.com) signed on as a cover designer, and became a friend. You're sure to fall in love, indeed. This journey would not have been possible without the example and the teaching of Joanna Penn at www.thecreativepenn.com. I am delighted, Joanna, to add this volume to your list of books you have enabled. No doubt you will hit your one million mark any day now!

Readers are invited to listen to the
YOU'RE SURE TO FALL IN LOVE Playlist at
www.youresuretofallinlove.com

Bruce K Beck is both a writer and an accomplished chef. He is the author of **PRODUCE: A FRUIT AND VEGETABLE LOVERS' GUIDE**, which was called "gorgeous" by *The New York Times*, "a dazzler" by *Bon Appetit*, and "the most spectacular food book of the year" by *The Boston Globe*. His next book was **THE OFFICIAL FULTON FISH MARKET COOKBOOK**, which was called "invaluable" by Jacques Pépin, and "a treasure" by Irene Sax of *Newsday*. And Rex Reed said, ". . .you'll love this book. It's like a movie!"